POWDER RIVER RANGE

T0243639

A GREAT WESTERN DETECTIVE LEAGUE CASE

POWDER RIVER RANGE

PAUL COLT

THORNDIKE PRESS
A part of Gale, a Cengage Company

LIBRARY OF CONGRESS CIP DATA ON FILE.
CATALOGUING IN PUBLICATION FOR THIS BOOK
IS AVAILABLE FROM THE LIBRARY OF CONGRESS.

ISBN-13: 979-8-88578-942-4 (softcover alk. paper)

Published in 2023 by arrangement with Paul Colt.

POWDER RIVER RANGE

PROLOGUE

Buffalo
Johnson County
Wyoming Territory
1880

Banks, Maddie O'Rourke thought as she stepped out of a blustery Wyoming wind into the dull sepia glow of late afternoon lobby. Polished plank floor, barred teller cages, neatly arranged in a row. A couple of sober looking bankers, wearing dignified dark suits, one black the other an adventurous dark blue. Both seated at meticulous desks devoid of anything save the paper at hand for the moment. They flanked a massive steel vault door like bookends, fenced off from routine customer transactions behind a decorative low wooden railing. They must have a blueprint somewhere all banks are required follow. This one interchangeable with every other bank she had ever entered. She crossed the lobby, approaching the gate. The older, black suited banker on the right was engaged in some business with a young couple. Blue suit the younger, looked up from some ledger as she approached.

"May I help you?"

She caught the familiar look of the effect she had on some men. She presented a fine figure of a woman, with wholesome good looks, waves of velvet auburn hair, and a flawless peaches and cream complexion splashed lightly across the bridge of an upturned nose with girlish golden freckles.

"I'd like to open an account."

He stood offering one of those "pleased to be of service" smiles all bankers seem to perfect along with the ability to summon it at will. He rounded his desk to hold the gate open for her.

"Please, step inside and have a seat. Artimis Atwater at your service."

He offered a limp soft hand she accepted.

"Madeline O'Rourke."

"Pleased to meet you . . ."

"Mrs. Madeline O'Rourke." That she was a widow served no purpose to the conversation. The illusion of marriage put the banker's look to rest.

"Very well then, Mrs. O'Rourke. What brings you to Buffalo?"

"I understand the cattle business is booming here. Such situations breed opportunity."

"I must say, you don't look like a rancher."

"I'm not. I'll be looking for business or investment opportunities to profit from those engaged in the cattle trade."

"Investment, then are we talking a rather substantial account?"

"Substantial to me."

"Well let's get started then."

He extracted a numbered card from a desk drawer, arranged it on his blotter, and took pen in hand.

"And will the account be held jointly between you and Mr. O'Rourke?"

Damn, should have seen that question coming. "My name only, Mr. O'Rourke passed on a number of years ago."

"I'm so sorry. Madeline O'Rourke," he scratched across the top of the card. "Address?"

"I've only just arrived in town and have yet to locate a permanent residence."

"I understand. Just let us know when you are settled. And now the amount you wish to deposit?"

"Nine-thousand-four hundred dollars."

"And how will the account be funded?"

Maddie drew a bank draft from her purse

and slid it across the desk.

Atwater studied it. "Drawn on City National Bank of Denver. Fine institution. Do you have an account there?"

"I do until this draft is credited to my account here."

"That may take a few days, but rest assured we will initiate a most expeditious collection procedure."

"I'm quite sure you will. Is there anything further you require of me?"

"Sign here." He slid the account card across the desk along with his pen.

Maddie signed. "Should you need to contact me before I locate permanent residence, you can reach me at the Johnson Hotel. You know it?"

"Finest hotel in Johnson County." He stood with that smile again. "Welcome to Buffalo, Mrs. O'Rourke, and thank you for entrusting your business to Bank of Buffalo."

She took the offered hand, *only bank in town.*

Leaving the bank, she came upon the young couple, having just concluded their meeting with old black suit. Buffeted by gusty wind the young woman had tears in her eyes.

"What do we do now?"

"I don't know," he said.

"I'm sorry, I couldn't help overhearing. I see something is wrong. Is there something I might help with?"

The young man shook his head. "Not unless you own a bank to compete with this one."

"Turn you down for a loan, did they?"

Both nodded. "We need it to stock our small ranch."

"If you don't mind my asking, how much do you need?"

"Eight hundred dollars, nine hundred if we could get it," he said.

"Secured by a mortgage lean on the property?"

"That's what we asked for."

"Madeline O'Rourke." She stuck out her hand. "I may be able to help."

"Are you serious, ma'am?"

"I am. I'll have to see the property first and we will need to work out the details."

"Dan Shaw," he extended his hand. "This is my wife, Susan."

"Pleased to meet you, ma'am," Susan said.

"Ma'am sounds so old. My friends call me Maddie. There's a café in the next block. Let's get out of this wind, have a cup of coffee, and get better acquainted."

11

■ ■ ■ ■

Nice young couple, Maddie thought lingering over her second cup of coffee with no place to go after the Shaws departed other than a lonely hotel room. Dan and Susan invited her to visit the ranch, which she agreed to do as soon as she had papers drawn for her purchase of a twenty percent interest in the enterprise. *Building a future together.* It looked like a recipe for happiness.

Happiness. She caught her reflection in her coffee. She counted herself a fugitive from happiness, alone in northern Wyoming. She'd been so comfortable behind the walls of her rules. Slowly he'd chipped away at them, daring her to take a chance. She did. Frightened of the risk of loss, she'd made certain of it. Choices. For better or worse they get made. She'd made hers. Now came the hard part. Living with it.

CHAPTER ONE

O'Rourke House
Denver
1911

I strolled along the pleasantly familiar tree-lined lane on a sunny warm Saturday bound for a certain stately Victorian a few blocks up the street. By way of introduction for those whose acquaintance I have not made before, my name is Robert Brentwood. I beg indulgence of those who may be familiar with this part of the story; but as we walk along, I should explain for the benefit of those new to these adventures. I am employed as a reporter for the *Denver Tribune,* though in this venture I've come to compile stories of the Great Western Detective League. The idea for this project first occurred to me when I stumbled on reports of this association of law enforcement professionals in the *Tribune* archives. Imagine my surprise when I discovered, quite by accident, the mastermind behind this storied network of crime fighters still alive and comfortably ensconced at the Shady Grove Rest Home and Convalescent Center. My nascent writing career seemed foreordained by the discovery.

As things came to pass, Colonel David J. Crook (U.S. Army Ret.) agreed to assist me in my ambition in return for . . . modest compensation. A bottle of contraband whiskey surreptitiously delivered each week at no small risk to my personal happiness. That too shall become apparent presently. In return we completed three stories dramatizing the extraordinary exploits of the Colonel's legendary organization. Well perhaps not yet legendary; it shall certainly be so before we are finished.

The Colonel and I struck up something of a, dare I say, fatherly relationship over his telling of these tales. Regrettably we lost him to the ravages of age two years ago already. I'll not deny I wept like a child at his passing. He could be curmudgeonly, sarcastic, and an impossible tease. We loved him, my Penny and me. We owed him much.

My Penny, Miss Penny O'Malley at the time, is now Mrs. Robert Brentwood as of our nuptials last year. She served as the Colonel's nurse at Shady Grove Rest Home and Convalescent Center. The Colonel took it upon himself to introduce my tongue-tied self to her when I couldn't bring myself to do so. In so doing he imparted an amazing possibility into my life. He did it out of the irascible conviction he might not live long enough to see me speak for myself. That, quintessentially, is the Colonel. He was an incorrigible interventionist who felt perfectly permitted to barge into our private affairs without regard to social convention or the least consideration for proper courtesy. Privacy and social convention were never a deterrent to his meddling. He did of course gain the desired result. As to our marriage I say again, we owe him much.

When the Colonel passed, I feared through my veil of tears, I might be forced to continue these stories without guidance. To my great surprise providence provided at his funeral. An old colleague appeared to pay his respects. I spotted Briscoe Cane at the Colonel's graveside. I didn't know him personally, though I well knew the prominent part he played in the work of the Great Western Detective League in the course of the league's many cases. Aside from a few years of age he rang true to the Colonel's description. Hickory hard frame of angular construction, features stitched in worn saddle leather. I ventured a speculation to introduce myself and was delighted to find my speculation correct.

He'd taken up residence here in Denver at this very house. We shall presently begin again the next chapter in telling the exploits of the Great Western Detective League. Before we do, I should like you to meet him as the Colonel introduced him to me. The Colonel recruited him in the matter of a robber fugitive known as Sam Bass. As the Colonel told me of Cane's recruitment, he used his considerable facility with information to impress Cane with what he knew of him.

"I know, for example, you favor a pair of fine-balanced bone-handled blades, one sheathed behind that .44 holster rig and the other in your left boot. I know you can draw and throw with either hand fast enough to silently defeat another man's gun draw."

"I know you are equally fast with that Colt and a .41 caliber Forehand & Wadsworth Bull Dog rigged for cross draw at your back. Some consider a spur trigger pocket pistol the weapon of choice for a whore. Such a notion would sadly misestimate your use of it. Those that do, seldom do so for long."

"I also know you carry a Henry rifle and I'm told you can pluck out a man's eye at a

thousand paces. I know that when called for, you possess a master craftsman's skills with explosives. In my humble opinion, were it not for the staunch religious foundation afforded by your upbringing you might have had a more prosperous career as an assassin than the one you have as a bounty hunter."

Cane resisted the Colonel's invitation at first. The Colonel, as he soon learned, could be quite persuasive. In the end Cane agreed to join the Colonel's Great Western Detective League. I doubt he'd admit it, but I suspect he never looked back. Ah here we are.

O'Rourke House stands in the middle of the block, neatly bordered by tended gardens tucked behind a wrought iron fence. A central gate opened to a walkway leading three steps up to a broad porch fronting the length of the house. Lace-curtained leaded glass windows added a welcoming touch to polished wood double doors. I tapped the heavy brass door knocker.

Angela Fitzwalter, a pleasantly attractive older woman, responded to my knock. We'd become acquainted over Mr. Cane's telling of the case of the Assassin's Witness last year. She took great interest in the planning of our wedding. In due course I came to puzzle over the odd nature of the relationship between the proprietress of O'Rourke and her confirmed bachelor tenant, perhaps not as confirmed as appearances postured.

"Robert! So good to see you. And Penny, is she well? Such a lovely bride she made. You simply must tell me everything of your honeymoon trip." She caught herself at the last. "Well, certainly not everything." Touch of pink on her cheek. "Now don't just stand there. Come in, come in."

The foyer smelled of floor wax with a hint of fresh baked bread.

"Have a seat in the parlor. I'll call him."

I took a comfortable chair in a handsomely appointed, stiffly formal, Victorian parlor. Mrs. Fitzwalter climbed the stairs. Presently I overheard.

"Briscoe dear, Robert is here."

See what I mean about nature of their relationship?

He followed her down the stairs creak by creak. I rose.

"Robert, good to see you. I half thought you might give up on the weekly telling of these tales for the charms of that lovely wife of yours."

"Charms? What would you know of charms?" Angela pecked at him.

"Why my dear you know I have a keen appreciation of charm. It is why I am so very fond of yours."

"Fond is it? And I'm not your dear."

"Not so anyone would know it."

I only marveled at the glint or twinkle she produced on command in her eye whenever they bantered. The pair of them *doth protest too much.*

"I shall leave you two to another of Briscoe's tall tales."

Off she harrumphed across foyer to the dining room and kitchen beyond.

He winked. "She listens you know."

"Do not!" Echoed the kitchen.

He tossed his head toward the dining room with a "see" smile, extending a hand.

I handed over his weekly bottle of Old Crow. We repaired to the parlor.

"Would you gentlemen care for a cup of coffee?" Angela called from the kitchen. "I wouldn't want you to start on that whiskey. Moderation you know."

"What whiskey?"

"You and I both know very well what whiskey."

"Afraid she does, Robert," he said under his breath.

"A cup of coffee would be very nice, Angela dear."

"Moderation has been a house rule going back to Maddie O'Rourke's time. Rules are

19

made to be broken."

He glanced toward the kitchen, conspiratorially. "Angela's alright when she lets her hair down. Don't tell her I said so. Her judgment can be affected by a couple fingers of good whiskey."

Mrs. Fitzwalter returned with two steaming cups of coffee she set on the side tables with a sidelong glance at Briscoe. "Your attempts at fraternization in no way affect my judgment. Call if you need anything." She returned to the kitchen.

We took seats.

Briscoe scratched a whiskered chin in need of a shave. "Now where exactly did we last leave ourselves?"

"Who was the man with you at the wedding? I know I don't know him, but something about him seemed so familiar."

"Should. You've written books about him."

"Beau Longstreet?"

"None other."

I made an effort to absorb such startling information. "And the woman?"

Briscoe smiled. "I told you it was a long story."

I drew out my pad, moistening the point of my pencil on the tip of my tongue.

"It all started back at the beginning before the real trouble started."

"Here we go beginning in riddles."

"Of course. Riddles you know are the stuff of detective work. Now let's see . . ."

CHAPTER TWO

Sheriff's Office
Cheyenne
Wyoming Territory

Sheriff Habb Tyler sat at his sun-splashed desk, a steaming cup of morning coffee at his elbow and a stack of wanted dodgers on his desk. He sifted through the stack searching for any that matched notices received from Great Western Detective League offices. These he would attend to first. If the league had a line on a case, it increased chances something might be afoot with opportunity for bonus compensation. The visitor bell brought him up from his reading. Charles Weston cut the dignified figure of a well to do lawyer, which he was. Pillar of the community with a furrowed brow didn't bode well.

"Good morning, Charles. You don't have the look of a social call."

"Morning, Habb. No, I'm sure I don't."

"Have a seat."

Weston took the offered chair.

"Now what's on your mind, Charles?"

"I believe you know I sit on the board of the Cattle Growers Bank."

Tyler nodded.

"I also represent the board on the bank's loan committee. As you know, the board hired Preston Prather to the position of bank president last year. He came to us highly recommended with impeccable qualifications. Of late I have had some concern over the quality of credits to which Preston is willing to extend loans."

Tyler raised a hand. "Credits?"

"The creditworthiness of the borrower and the quality of assets pledged against repayment of the loan. It helps judge the risk of a loan and the capacity of the borrower to repay it."

"So, you're saying the loans might carry a higher risk of default."

"Exactly."

"Go on."

"At loan committee yesterday afternoon, Preston presented a credit proposal to extend a loan of twenty-five thousand dollars to one Augustus McNabb with the loan to be secured by ranchland, buildings, and herds owned by Mr. McNabb. The holdings appear substantial on paper, but the loan amount gives me pause. If a loan of that size were to default, it could easily put the bank at risk."

"If the loan is too risky, can't the board simply step in?"

"In theory, yes, but Preston has done a masterful job of ingratiating himself to the directors. Some might call it a honeymoon with those inclined to trust the man's experience and credentials. I agonized over the situation last night and came to the conclusion we are in need of some objective oversight. And that is why I am here."

Tyler rocked his barrel-backed chair, making a steeple of fingertips at his chin. "Who is Augustus McNabb? I've never heard of him. With ranch holdings that large, you'd think I would have."

"I've never heard of him either. We have only Preston's representations to go on."

"Do you know where this ranch is located?"

"I saw the schedule of holdings and the valuation presented. All of which seemed reasonable as far as the paper goes, but as to the exact location, I don't know."

"There are ways to rob a bank that don't involve a holdup."

"That's what I'm afraid of, Habb."

24

"I'll be honest with you, Charles, when it comes to bank robbery, I'm better suited to the holdup variety. If I start nosing around it will be visible to everyone. If Prather and McNabb have some sort of fraud in mind, we'll need help to bring it to light."

"What do you have in mind?"

"I am affiliated with a law enforcement network known as the Great Western Detective League. It is an association of law enforcement officers who cooperate in criminal cases that cross jurisdictions."

"Never heard of it."

"Most people haven't and that's why they are perfect for assisting in a situation just such as this."

"Do you think they will help?"

"The association takes cases where there is opportunity for reward or recovery. Given the risk you describe, I suspect the board would entertain a reward for recovery should the need arise."

"Let's hope it doesn't come to that, but should it, I'm sure the board would consider it."

"If you agree, I can get a wire off to Colonel Dave Crook, the league superintendent, to see what he suggests."

"A law enforcement league headed by a man named Crook. On that I defer to your judgment, Habb. At least I'll have the peace of mind, knowing something is being done."

"I'll get a wire off to Colonel Crook and let you know what he says."

"Thanks, Habb."

Great Western Detective League Offices
Denver

On a bright sunny morning the freckle-faced, red-haired young scamp in shabby overhauls and ragged red-checked shirt who ran telegrams for Western Union rolled up to the league office and hopped down from his velocipede. He propped it up against the hitch rack, skipped across the boardwalk, and cracked the door to the tune of the visitor's bell, splashed in sunlight. Longstreet met him at the door, exchanging the telegram for a quarter. He knocked on the frame of Colonel Crook's open office door.

"For you." He handed the foolscap across Crook's desk and turned to go.

Crook tore open the envelope and scanned. "Hold on a second, Beau."

Longstreet paused in the doorway. "Trouble?"

"Do these things ever come with birthday greetings?"

"Is it your birthday?"

"You'll never know. No, it's from Habb

Tyler in Cheyenne. He's got a case of suspected bank fraud on his hands. He'd like a little help."

"What are you planning to do?"

Crook slid the telegram back across his desk. "Me? Nothing. I'm sending you up to Cheyenne to do a little undercover work."

"My work is nothing?"

"No. Just undercover."

"I'll catch the morning train."

O'Rourke House
Denver
1911

I shook out a writer's cramp, sensing our session finished by the golden light of late afternoon.

"I caught but a brief glimpse of him at the wedding. I know he was old South and a shirttail cousin to the famous Confederate General James Longstreet. I know he served, reaching the rank of captain. I know he got his investigative start at Pinkerton and that you recruited him for Colonel Crook after the two of you tracked down Sam Bass on opposite sides of that case. But what was he like back in the day?"

"Tall, well made, handsome devil, dripping with southern charm. Damn fine investigator and competent man in a tough

27

situation. That said he might have been at his best, turning the head of some unsuspecting young lady. At least that's the way it was until Maddie O'Rourke came along."

"We know that didn't end well after her run-in with El Anillo. What happened after she left?"

"He nursed a broken heart for a spell. He was better at breaking hearts than mending his own. Then Samantha Maples showed up in town."

"Old flame. I remember her from the Pinkerton side of the bogus bond case and the phony jewel mine fraud."

"The very same. She never turned down the heat when it came to Longstreet. Neither did Beau, until Maddie came along. When Maddie left, Samantha helped him put his broken heart back in order."

"I see. Then who was the woman with him at our wedding?"

Briscoe smiled. "Like I said, it's a long story."

"Next week then?"

"I see I'm to be treated to more riddles. Next week then?"

He patted Old Crow. "Next week."

CHAPTER THREE

Sheriff's Office
Cheyenne

Rain lashed Sixteenth Street, soaking Longstreet on the two-block walk from the depot. He ducked inside the sheriff's office. "Sheriff Tyler?" Longstreet made it a guess worthy of a professional investigator. Man, wearing a star seated at the lone desk in a small sheriff's office.

"I am. How can I help?"

"Beau Longstreet, Great Western Detective League. Far as I know, I'm here to help you."

Tyler rose, extending his hand. "Been expecting you. Thanks for coming. Have a seat and please, call me Habb."

"Much obliged."

"How was your trip up from Denver?"

"Union Pacific makes that run a piece of cake these days. Those two-day stage ordeals are a distant and painful memory. Best part of that trip was, it's over. Suspected bank fraud doesn't tell us much. Can you fill in the blanks?"

"Some. You'll want to talk to Charles Weston. He's the bank director who brought the suspicion to my attention. He sits on the board and loan committee of the Cattle Growers Bank. About a year ago the bank hired a new president. Gent's name is Preston Prather. Came highly recommended, sterling credentials according to those who know about such things."

"Where'd he come from?"

"Don't know. You'll have to ask Charles."

"Go on."

"Prather is proposing the bank extend a substantial loan to a man named Augustus McNabb. The loan to be secured by McNabb's ranchland, buildings, and stock. Charles is concerned for several reasons. Nobody knows McNabb. The holdings, pledged as security, exist on paper. Nobody knows where the ranch is located. The loan is large enough to threaten the stability of the bank, were it to default."

"How much?"

"Twenty-five thousand."

"Serious money."

"It is and all of it supported by the word of one man, Prather."

"Weston can't be the only director concerned. Has he talked with the others?"

Tyler nodded. "They're all impressed with Prather's qualifications and the work he has done over the past year. That's another of Charles's concerns. Prather has worked real hard to befriend board members and gain their confidence."

"Hmm. I see the concern. So far all it adds up to is the prospect of a risky loan. A risk nobody seems worried about other than Mr. Weston. You're right, I do need to speak to him."

"His law office is a block north of Sixteenth on Ransom. Ransom is a block east of here. I'd take you, but might be best if we weren't seen together."

"Good idea. I'll keep you posted as the situation warrants."

Mercifully, the rain stopped. Rumpled gray felt cloud scudded east on a brisk Wyoming wind. Longstreet swung north on Ransom. The sign lettered in gold leaf on the window glass read Attorney at Law. Longstreet entered. Richly polished wood appointed the interior, every bit as elegant as the sign out front. A young clerk looked up from a thick leather-bound volume open on his desk.

"May I help you?"

"I'd like to see Mr. Weston, please."

"Is he expecting you?"

"I believe so."

"Who may I say is calling?"

"Beau Longstreet, Great Western Detective League."

"Send him in, Brad."

The anonymous voice came from an open office door. Brad gestured the way in. A distinguished gentleman in a dark suit, graying at the temples, rose from his desk in greeting. He extended his hand.

"Charles Weston, Mr. Longstreet. Glad to have you here." Handshakes exchanged. "Please, have a seat. How can I help?"

"Sheriff Tyler filled me in on the situation regarding the loan in question. I have a couple of questions for you. Habb tells me Prather is relatively new to the bank and that he came to you highly recommended. Where did he come from?"

"His curriculum vitae listed his last position as one in a senior lending capacity at Bank of Omaha."

"Did you or any other board member contact Bank of Omaha?"

"He presented a glowing letter of recommendation from the bank president. That was deemed sufficient reference for our purposes."

"Where is McNabb's ranch located?"

"North Platte, according to the loan application."

"Has anyone inspected the property to verify the claimed collateral?"

"Preston represented he had."

"Why would a rancher from North Platte solicit a loan from a bank in Cheyenne?"

"I questioned that too. Given the size of the loan, you need a bank big enough to underwrite it. By rail, Cheyenne and Omaha are the choices. We're told McNabb knew Preston from his time at Bank of Omaha and followed him to Cheyenne with his business."

"Convenient how neatly all that ties together."

"That along with all the admiration Preston has cultivated with the board explains why I'm the only one questioning this transaction. What do you plan to do about it?"

"Three things come to mind. I'll wire our league members in Omaha and North Platte."

"League members?"

"The Great Western Detective League is an association of law enforcement officers who cooperate in investigations that cross jurisdictions. The league member in Omaha can verify Prather's credentials. The member in North Platte can identify the McNabb ranch holdings to give us a reading that doesn't rely on Prather's word."

"Very helpful. That makes two. You said three things came to mind. What's next?"

"Another loan."

"Another loan?"

"Yes, sir. I make a loan application similar to the McNabb terms. Let's see if Prather is willing to make that loan again."

"Very clever."

"I'll need some help."

"How so?"

"We need to find a ranch in the area I can 'borrow' with an accepted offer to purchase at a sum equaling the amount of the McNabb loan. We then secure the loan with a pledge of the real property. That way, Prather can inspect the property and render a decision. If he approves the loan and everything else checks out, we'll have a pretty good idea the McNabb loan is legitimate."

"What do you think will happen?"

"We don't deal in speculation. We deal in facts."

CHAPTER FOUR

Buffalo

Buffalo lay in the Powder River basin in the eastern foothills of the Big Horn Mountains. The town sprawled along Clear Creek with town center clustered along Main Street from south to north. Fort Street headed west out of town to Fort McHenry. A block south, Fetterman cut Buffalo's commercial center from west to east.

Maddie purchased a two-bedroom white-washed, clapboard home set behind a white picket fence on West Hart Street a few blocks north of town center off Main Street. She settled into her new surroundings, planting a garden cultivated in prairie flower beds along the front of the house, and beside the walkway between gate and front porch with a lovely swing.

This day, she donned a gingham sunbonnet for the short walk into town. She rented a cabriolet drawn by a handsome blood bay for the drive northeast out of town to visit the Shaw's ranch. The bay jogged along at an easy gait. Grassland rolled by, dotted here and there with grazing cattle under a bright blue sky.

The Shaw homestead sat on a bend in Clear Creek. A small cabin along with a barn and corral nestled in the shade of a small grove of cottonwood trees. As Maddie turned up the lane winding to the cabin, Susan Shaw stood in the yard talking with a mounted rider. She turned, shading her eyes at Maddie's approach. Recognizing her she waved. Maddie drew the bay's lines to a halt.

"Mrs. O'Rourke, what a pleasant surprise."

"Hello, Susan, and please, you know, call me Maddie." She stepped out of the carriage, dropping the tie-down in front of the bay.

"Maddie, meet our neighbor Liza Quint. Liza, Maddie O'Rourke is the person who helped us get started on our ranch."

Liza Quint was a big-boned angular woman, weather-featured and dressed as a man in her work clothes. She sat astride a pink-rimmed blue-eyed piebald well matched to her rider's confirmation. "Pleased to make your acquaintance, Maddie, if I may call you that."

"Of course, Liza. Where is your place?"

"East of here."

"Liza has been ranching in Johnson County for years," Susan said. "She has given us a wealth of good advice."

"Nice of you to say so, Susan. You know what they say about free advice."

"What?"

"Worth what you pay for it." She smiled a crooked yellow grin, stained by an occasional chaw.

"If that's so, Dan and I have enjoyed a great bargain."

"Well time for me to mosey on home and make sure none of them big boys has picked on my herd. Pleased to make your acquaintance, Maddie. Welcome to Buffalo."

"Thank you, Liza."

She swung the piebald away, picking up a lope to the east.

"Where's Dan?"

"Out checking our herd."

"What did Liza mean by big boys picking on her herd?"

"Big ranchers consider all this land public grazing. They had the run of it, before the Homestead Act allowed folks like us to settle here. Most of them aren't happy about it. All that cattle baron influence is cozied up to the governor's office in Cheyenne. Johnson County ranchers are an irritant to them. Their herds mingle with ours out there." She swept an arm east, north to south. We make sure to keep close track on what is ours. Care for some lemonade to get out of this heat?"

"Sounds delightful."

Law Office
Cheyenne

"Go right in, Mr. Longstreet. Mr. Weston is expecting you."

"Thanks. Brad is it?"

"Yes, sir."

Weston sat at his desk, backlit in bright sunshine.

"I got your message at the hotel," Longstreet said. "Have you got something for me?"

"I do." He slid a document across the desk.

Longstreet took a seat and read. The document set out terms for a bill of sale, conditioned on the buyer, Longstreet, obtaining financing. "Who's Davis Chesterfield?"

"One of the biggest ranchers in Wyoming. Davis is a client. He agreed to help us when I explained it will be used to audit lending policy at Cattle Growers Bank."

"Now who's clever?"

"It is an audit of sorts and an audit of this nature must necessarily be confidential."

"What's the best way to approach Prather?"

"I've given that some thought too. Preston knows I represent Davis. I will send him a note that I am handling the sale for him. I'll ask him to meet you at the Cattlemen's Club after the bank closes today. The Cattlemen's Club is frequented by the rich and powerful in this state. It's the place to see and be seen. It sets you apart. The invitation will be irresistible to Prather's burnished opinion of himself. Just being seen there says you are someone important."

Longstreet nodded. "Mr. Weston, did you ever think of going into criminal investigation? You have a flare for it."

"Nice of you to say so. We in the legal profession are sometimes consumers of the work done by investigators. We gain some appreciation for the work."

"Pleasure working with you."

Omaha, Nebraska
"Telegram, Sheriff."

Cheyenne
Verify employment and reference for Preston Prather, Bank of Omaha president's office.
Advise B. Longstreet, Great Western Detective League

North Platte, Nebraska
"Just came in, Sheriff."

Cheyenne
Identify and inspect ranch holdings of Augustus McNabb.
Advise B. Longstreet, Great Western Detective League

O'Rourke House
Denver
1911

Lengthening late afternoon shadows suggested our session coming to an end. I closed my notebook, tucking my pencil in the binding.

"Enough for today?" Cane said.

"I think so. It seems like Longstreet is headed for an early resolution of the case. Do we have a book here?"

"I told you it's a long story."

"It all began before the beginning, according to your riddle, right?"

40

"Something like that. So how is wedded bliss?"

"Blissful indeed. All the more so when we locate a new home."

"New home's a big step."

"It is, but we judge it a necessary step to properly providing for a family."

"Family. Even bigger step."

"Tends to follow from the first big step, marriage."

"I suppose it does."

"Family?" Angela called from the stairway rounding the turn post to the parlor. "Is somebody in a family way?"

I felt my cheeks redden. "Only in a planning way."

"So exciting to be young and in love. So many new beginnings."

"Robert and Penny are looking for a house."

"My, that's exciting too. May I ask where you are looking?"

"We hope to find something affordable within walking distance of the *Tribune*. Unfortunately, the affordable part is something of a challenge. Property that close to town is more expensive."

"Be patient, Robert. Something is bound to turn up," Angela said.

I rose to leave. "Next week then?"

"See you then."

I let myself out.

Cane lifted his chin to Angela.

"How much of this do you manage to listen to?"

"Some. Most entertaining conversation in the house you know. Like getting a preview of the book and learning something of your nefarious past in the bargain."

"Our conversation isn't entertaining?"

"Conversation or banter?"

"Keeps us on our toes."

"Is that it?"

"Is. And I'll have you know my past has more to do with righting nefarious purpose than committing it."

"So, you say. As in moderation, I shall be the judge of that."

"Remind me to remember, you're listening."

"Why so? Would you tell a different tale for my benefit?"

"Wouldn't think of it."

"Likely leave out all your female conquests."

"Left all that to Longstreet."

"I'm sure you did."

"You wouldn't be jealous, now would you?"

"Jealous? Of what? Preposterous!"

"Sounds like jealousy to me."

"Remind me to remember you're listening."

"That makes two of us."

"Your hearing isn't that good."

"Yours is good enough for both of us."

CHAPTER FIVE

Denver
1911

We rented a small apartment over a mercantile to house us after the wedding. It was a decent size one-room affair with every aspect of life rolled in together. Cooking was limited to a small wood-burning stove, with food preparation and consumption sharing the same table. Built in wardrobes passed for closet space. The only furnishing we purchased was a new bed. Beyond that a couple of decrepit chairs, side table, and oil lamp provided by the landlord completed the furnishings. The store owner lived in it initially. Having no further need of it after he purchased a proper house, he began renting it. The best to be said for it was the modest rent allowed us to save for a home of our own.

Proper house. We saved. Royalty checks from book sales went into the "house account." The moment we had enough of a down payment to qualify for a mortgage we started to look. A disappointing process. Homes we might afford were found outside of town. Those that suited my work location, went beyond our means.

I climbed the back stairs to the apartment where I was greeted to a fragrant, sizzling scent. My Penny stood at the stove, stirring.

"Hi handsome," she said over her shoulder at the sound of the latch.

"Hi yourself." I crossed the room, spun her about at the hips, and kissed her soundly. The moment melted. She pulled back. "The potatoes," she protested at the back of her throat. "They'll . . . burn."

I surrendered her lips. "Appetizer. I'll see you later for dessert."

She took to her stirring. "How was Briscoe today?"

"Himself, as always. I declare I'm stumped to understand how he and Angela get on. Good natured bickering hardly seems a way of life."

"Good natured. Old friends. They're comfortable with it. We're likely too young to understand. How is the book coming?"

"It's a bit of a riddle."

"Aren't all investigations?"

"They are. This one seems rather cut and

dried. More of a short story than a book."

"Did you mention that to Briscoe?"

"I did. He says it's a long story."

"Then trust him. He hasn't steered you wrong yet. Now wash up. Supper will be on in a moment."

"What's for dessert?"

"Surprise me."

"I plan to."

Actually, I hadn't planned on surprising her. It was Penny surprised me on our honeymoon. She had a playful side to her I'd credited to her sense of humor. Turns out there is more to it than that. Delightfully more to it. Victorian mores tend to be quite straitlaced. Turns out they can be unlaced too. A surprise for dessert indeed. I set my imagination to imagining.

O'Rourke House
Denver
1911

The following Saturday afternoon Angela greeted my knock at the door.

"And how is Robert today?"

"Just fine, thank you."

"Any progress on house hunting?"

"I'm afraid not."

"Don't be discouraged. The right thing just hasn't come along yet. These things

46

happen in their own time. Have a seat in the parlor. I'll tell Briscoe you're here."

I did so as she climbed halfway up the stairs to call.

"Briscoe dear, Robert is here."

Briscoe dear. I suppressed a smile. Is it possible the old bachelor could be smitten at this stage in the game?

She led the way back down the stairs to the kitchen. Briscoe turned the banister post to the parlor.

"Punctual as usual, Robert. How was your week?"

"Busy. The Colorado State Democrat convention was in town. I got the assignment to cover it. Long days and late nights."

"Scoundrels. All politicians in my experience. How did your bride take having you out 'til all hours?"

"Puts food on the table until your stories allow me to write for a living."

"You do write for a living."

"There's a difference between writing what you are told to write about and writing about something you have a passion for."

"And you have a passion for the Great Western Detective League?"

"Hasn't let me down so far."

"Yes, we have hit on a few good stories. The Colonel had quite the reputation as a law enforcement officer. Interesting, often spectacular cases tended to come our way because of it."

"And you had clever officers to deal with those cases, which I'm sure only served to further the league's reputation."

"Yes, I suppose there is that."

"Something of an accomplishment what with Pinkerton forever lurking in the shadows."

"Merely added spice. Samantha Maples for Longstreet, Sir Reggie for me."

"Kingsley?"

"The very same. Slippery that one."

"Keeps the stories interesting. Perhaps we should begin."

"Let's see then. Where were we?"

I consulted my notes. "Longstreet was about to meet the banker, Prather."

"Ah yes . . ."

Cattlemen's Club
Cheyenne
Money. Money and power, you can smell 'em. Longstreet took in the statements of wealth and privilege that made the Cattlemen's Club the Cattlemen's Club. Spacious room appointed in elegant conversational groupings upholstered in rich tan leather and dark green velvet, arranged around a

massive fireplace along one wall. Polished pegged wooden floor. Mirrored full bar stretched along the far wall with billiard and card tables at the end opposite the fireplace. Longstreet sidled up to the bar near the seating area. He ordered whiskey from a portly bartender in starched linen, sporting a waxed mustache. From here he could keep an eye out for Prather and take in a feel for the hum of conversation.

A pair of well-dressed cattle barons sat nearby.

"Damn Homestead Act started it all."

"Small operators, squatting all over Powder River basin. Piddling little herds compete for graze and water on open range. Public grazing land rightfully belongs to us."

"To make matters worse, most of 'em would rather rustle my stock than grow their own."

"Johnson County may be the worst of the lot. Folks in Buffalo own the county. Law up there ain't fit for cow chips."

"Sure 'nuf look after their own. Even that rustlin' whore Liza Quint."

Just then a man in a dark blue suit came in. He flicked open a gold pocket watch, glancing around the room. Longstreet shoved off the bar and crossed the room.

"Mr. Prather?"

49

"Mr. Longstreet?"

"Pleased to make your acquaintance."

"Charles's note suggested you are interested in financing purchase of Davis Chesterfield's ranch holdings."

"I am."

"That's one of the largest ranches in Wyoming. Impressive. Shall we have a seat and talk it over?"

"The corner card table looks quiet."

"It does."

Prather led the way. Something of a nondescript fellow. Mild mannered, quiet, thoughtful, steady demeanor suited to a banker. He took a seat, motioning Longstreet to do the same.

"So how much financing are we talking about?"

Longstreet drew the accepted offer from his inside coat pocket and slid it across the table. Prather fitted a pair of wire-rimmed glasses over his nose and read.

"Twenty-five thousand secured by a first mortgage on the ranch holdings. I am generally familiar with the ranch. We shall have to do a detailed inspection. If that bears up to the risk, we will propose the loan to the board for consideration."

"How long might that take?"

"Do you have a detailed schedule of the assets?"

"Not yet."

"We shall require one for verification."

"I see. I'll have Charles speak with Mr. Chesterfield about providing one. How long will it take to verify the schedule once you have it?"

"A holding of this size, at least two and possibly three weeks."

"In the meantime, preliminarily at least and subject to confirming the value, is this a transaction you can take to the board?"

"Taking it to the board is easy. Getting a loan of this size approved may be another matter."

"I'm a busy man, Mr. Prather. If I'm wasting my time, say so."

"I am only being cautious, Mr. Longstreet. Give me a few days to consult with my colleagues. If you can provide the schedule, I can give you a preliminary opinion."

Bank of Omaha

Bank president Miles Tate had no need to look at his watch. Cashier Tom Post left his desk promptly at a quarter of three to supervise balancing the cash drawers in preparation for closing. A familiar figure

51

crossed the lobby toward Tate's desk. *What might this portend?*

"Afternoon, Sheriff. What brings you by?"

"Afternoon, Miles. Just following up on a routine inquiry."

"How may we help?"

"What can you tell me about a former employee," the sheriff consulted his notes. "A gentleman by the name of Preston Prather. Know him?"

"I do. Preston got himself in some sort of trouble?"

"Can't say. All I was asked was to verify his employment."

"Preston worked here for a time . . ."

Register of Deeds
North Platte

Sheriff Reliable Kincaid ambled down a dimly lit courthouse hallway to a cramped cluttered back office at the end of the hall. Emmet Herman, County Registrar of Deeds, sat at a small desk piled high with ledgers and folders. A mouse of a man, he wore wire-rimmed spectacles, a green eyeshade, and garters holding up the sleeves to his spindle-like arms.

"Afternoon, Emmet."

"Sheriff. I'd offer you a cup of coffee though I suspect this isn't a social call."

"Not social. Just routine."

"What can I do for you?"

"Need to verify the landholdings of Augustus McNabb."

"Hmm." Herman scratched the stubble on his chin. "Must be before my time. Let me check the files . . ."

CHAPTER SIX

Stock Growers Bank
Cheyenne

Prather sat at his desk with a customer when Longstreet arrived at the bank. He waited in the lobby for the banker to finish his business. When the customer rose to leave, Prather motioned Longstreet to his desk.

"Mr. Longstreet, please have a seat. I presume you are here in regard to your loan application."

"I am. Has the board had a chance to review it?"

"I'm afraid that won't be necessary. After reviewing the schedule of assets, I cannot recommend approval of your request."

"I don't understand. The schedule we provided certainly supports the value of the loan. I realize inspection is needed to verify it. Why would you turn the loan down sight unseen?"

"A holding of that size can become illiquid

should the borrower default. Recovery can be slow with no current return to the bank."

"You assume the loan will default."

"I assume nothing, Mr. Longstreet. The business of prudent lending merely anticipates contingencies. In this case, I judge liquidity risk unacceptable. Now if you will excuse me, I have another customer waiting."

Dismissed, Longstreet turned to the gate, opening the low railing to the lobby as Prather called behind him.

"Mr. McNabb, right this way please."

Timely Longstreet thought, crossing the lobby past a broad-shouldered man in a black suit. A gusty Wyoming wind greeted him out on Sixteenth Street. He took the boardwalk east to Ransom and a block north.

Law Office

Weston was meeting with a client when Longstreet arrived. He cooled his heels thirty minutes before the lawyer could see him.

"Turned it down without so much as inspecting the property."

"Did he give you a reason?"

"Something about a property that size being . . . what was the word he used, ill-

55

something in the event of a default."

"Illiquid."

"That's it."

"Perhaps so, but that could also be true of the loan to McNabb. None of this does anything to lessen my concern over Preston's stewardship of the bank."

"Your concern seems well placed."

"The question is what to do next."

"We haven't heard anything of our inquiries in Omaha and North Platte."

"Yes, there is that. Perhaps there is one more thing we can do. As Davis's legal counsel, I suggest we confront Preston directly. It may force his hand."

"You sure you were never an investigator, Mr. Weston?"

Weston flipped open his pocket watch. "After three. We'll have to see about that tomorrow."

"I'll be by first thing in the morning," Longstreet said, rising to go.

Cattle Growers Bank
Friday Morning
Longstreet accompanied Weston to the bank the next morning, arriving promptly at nine o'clock for the bank opening. The lobby stood quiet at the onset of the business day. A tawny glow of polished wood lightly

scented in paper, ink, and currency. As they entered the lobby Weston glanced at Beau.

"Let me take the lead on this."

Longstreet nodded.

Prather sat at his desk, running a column of figures on a ledger sheet, a steaming cup of coffee at his elbow.

"Preston, a word if I may?"

"Have a seat, Charles. Mr. Longstreet, good morning."

They took the seats drawn up before Prather's desk.

"I presume you are here in regard to Mr. Longstreet's loan application."

"We are. Why was the loan not presented to the board?"

"I judged it too risky."

"How so?"

"As I explained to Mr. Longstreet yesterday, it is the liquidity risk of a holding that large. Buyers for that security don't grow on trees. Should the loan default, the bank could find itself in possession of a nonperforming asset absorbing a substantial amount of capital for an indefinite period of time."

"And how is that different from terms of another loan with which I am familiar?"

"The borrower in that case is well known to me. The loan closed yesterday with the first payment due at closing. The loan is current. It is an earning asset of the bank."

"Again, Preston, how is Mr. Longstreet's application any different?"

"The liquidity risk profiles may be similar. In one case we have been able to judge the risk acceptable. In this case we have not, though I saw no reason to verify the assets schedule. Mr. Longstreet pressed for a timely decision. I gave him one."

"Preston, you know the value of Davis's holdings will stand up to the valuation. Why would you turn down a credit of this quality?"

"As I told Mr. Longstreet. Liquidity risk."

"Liquidity risk is virtually identical in both credits. There has to be more to it than that."

"Character is also a judgment in lending, Charles. As a lawyer, you should well understand that."

"As a lawyer, I understand you are denying my client's borrower a loan over concern he is new to the community. As a director of this bank, I question turning away adequately secured new business."

"I stand by my decisions, Charles. If you wish to call my judgment into question with the board, I have no way to stop you. Now unless there is something further you wish

58

to discuss, I have a very busy day ahead of me."

"Good day then."

Back on the boardwalk Weston and Longstreet turned east to Ransom.

"When I left the bank yesterday, McNabb was Prather's next customer. He must have been there to close the loan."

"It would seem the bank may already be at risk."

"We'll know more once we hear from Omaha and North Platte. If Prather and McNabb check out as represented, at least you'll know where you stand."

"And if they don't?"

"We'd best know where to find them."

Johnson County

Wispy clouds drifted out of the mountains running east against an azure blue sky. Liza Quint and neighboring rancher Amos Miller rode slowly through a small mixed herd of grazing cattle, culling their brands away from the herd. Unbranded calves followed their mothers, sorting themselves for branding. Liza drew rein, shading her eyes with a gloved hand, looking south. Two riders approached at a lope.

"Amos," she pointed. "We got company. Know 'em?"

He let the riders close. "Don't."

The riders drew rein. "Let's have a look at them cattle."

"Who's askin?" Liza said.

"Wyoming Stock Growers Association stock detectives."

"That so. Says who?"

"Jack Black. This here's Red Gates. Have a look at them cows, Rusty."

The man with a rough red beard eased his mount forward.

"These cattle are ours. Mine are the Lazy Q brands. Rocking M's belong to Amos."

"They's unbranded calves mixed in here, Jack. Same as we thought."

Click. Black pulled his gun. "You two are coming with us. Get their guns, Rusty."

"What for?"

"Rustling, that's what for."

"Ain't no rustling to it. Them unbranded calves belong to their mamas. Even a stock detective knows that."

"Whose ranch is closest?"

"Mine," Liza said.

"Take us there."

"What for?"

"We aim to inspect the stock there and look for running irons."

"You're wastin' your time."

"Will see about that."

Lazy Q Ranch

The search of Liza Quint's ranch consisted of Gates ransacking the house and the barn while Black held Quint and Miller in the yard at gunpoint.

"Got anything, Rusty?"

Gates shook his head.

"Told you," Liza said. "No stock here but mine, let alone a runnin' iron. Now get the hell off my ranch."

"Her ranch," Black said. "Will ya listen to that. Rustler squatted on open range makin' demands of her betters."

"Betters my ass," Miller said. "You're nothin' but cattle baron's hired thugs."

"Hear that, Rusty? 'Nother rustler heard from. Seems like we should teach 'em both some manners."

"Manners hell. Teach 'em rustlin' don't pay. Send a message to the rest of their kind too."

"Mount up," Black ordered.

"Where we goin'?" Liza said.

"We're takin you into Buffalo to see the sheriff."

"What for. We ain't rustled nothin'."

"That'll be for the law to decide. Now mount up."

Mounted they crossed the yard to the Lazy Q gateway arch.

"That'll be far enough," Black said. "Use their own ropes, Rusty."

Gates threw two loops over the arch, tying them off on gateposts. He fit the loops over Liza's head, then Miller's.

"You'll never get away with this," Liza said. "It's murder."

"It's open range justice. Rustlin' is a hangin' offense."

"We ain't rustled nothin' and you know it."

"Tell it to the devil."

Gates slapped both horses on the rump, sending them out from under their riders. Feet kicking, both bodies swung free.

Cheyenne
Monday Morning

Longstreet sat before a stack of flapjacks with a rasher of bacon and a steaming cup of coffee. Morning sun streamed through the Rawlins House dining room window. The desk clerk crossed the room to his table.

"Telegram for you, Mr. Longstreet. Just came in." He handed over a small yellow envelope.

"Thank you." He tore it open and read.

Denver
North Platte Registrar of Deeds has no

62

record for Augustus McNabb–stop
  Prather briefly employed, Bank of
Omaha, position teller–stop
  Advise–stop
  Crook

Longstreet tossed his napkin on the table. Need to get this to Weston pronto. He rose, starting for the door, when a well-made young man wearing a deputy sheriff's star stopped him. Longstreet took him in. He bore the quiet confidence of a competent man. Close-cropped blond hair gave him boyish good looks, marred only by a small scar at the corner of his upper lip. Ice-blue slow eyes would not go lost on the ladies, though some men he faced might misestimate him.

"Mr. Longstreet?"

"Yes."

"Deputy Sheriff, Seth Adams."

"Trouble?"

"Yeah. Bank opened this morning. No sign of Prather. Sheriff's at the bank now. Sent me to fetch you."

Cattle Growers Bank
Longstreet led Adams into the bank. Charles Weston waited with Sheriff Tyler.

"What happened?" Longstreet said.

63

"Prather didn't show up to open the bank this morning. The cashier sent for me," Weston said. "I sent for the sheriff."

"Looks like we got our answer. I was on my way to see you when Seth came for me." Longstreet handed Weston the telegram.

"Sure, looks like our answer."

"Am I coming in late here?" Tyler said.

Weston handed him the telegram. "Where do we start?"

"The depot," Longstreet said.

CHAPTER SEVEN

Cheyenne Station

The station master shook his head. No one matching descriptions of Prather or Mc- Nabb purchased tickets over the weekend.

"I guess that rules out the train," Adams said.

"Doesn't," Longstreet said. "Rules out stupid."

"I don't follow."

"Board a train here, we'd have a trail. Where's the next closest stop?"

"Sidney."

"Eastbound."

"Westbound is Laramie."

"You catch on fast, Seth."

"Who takes which one?"

"Neither. We wire league officers at both stops to be on the lookout."

"So that's how this works."

"That's how this works."

Buffalo Bulletin

Local Ranchers Hanged
in Vigilante Justice

Local ranchers Liza Quint and Amos Miller found hanged from the gateway arch leading to Quint's Lazy Q ranch. Crudely scrawled notes pinned to their clothing branded them rustlers. Local authorities have no suspects, though Cattle Growers Association stock detectives known to be operating in the area are widely thought to be responsible.

Maddie set the paper down, her tea gone cold in the cup. Liza Quint. The Shaws' neighbor. Didn't strike her as a rustler. If she and Miller were caught rustling, why not let a court decide their fate? Why lynch them? Why?

Cheyenne Leader

Justice Served on
Johnson County Rustlers

Well known Johnson County rustlers Liza Quint and Amos Miller met their just ends at the end of a rope, as recently reported by the *Buffalo Bulletin.* Swift justice enacted by person or persons unknown . . .

66

Longstreet passed the paper across the sheriff's desk to Deputy Adams. "Sounds like the talk I overheard at the Cattlemen's Club the other day."

"Should. Cattlemen own the *Leader.*"

"Talk started with the politics of the Homestead Act. Were these folks rustlers or small ranchers homesteading on what used to be public grazing?"

"Small ranchers, rustlers, all the same to the big boys. Strung her up on her own gate for a reason."

"Those boys up to lynching?"

"That and more. You watch."

O'Rourke House
Denver
1911

I closed my notebook, marking our place with my pencil.

"I'm beginning to see what you mean by long story."

"Haven't steered you wrong yet, have I?"

"No, you haven't. Judging by that heavenly smell coming out of the kitchen, Angela's done right by you too."

"Apple pie," she called from the kitchen.

"Woman's got ears like a bat."

"I heard that, Briscoe Cane."

"Course you did. She does make a mighty

fine pie."

"Heard that too, dear."

"Now I'm dear."

"I best be heading home before this gets serious."

"In his wildest imagination. Would you like two pieces of pie to take home, Robert?"

"I couldn't put you to the trouble."

"No trouble."

"I'd do it if I were you."

"For my own good?"

"No. For the pie."

"Best advice he's given you all day, Robert. I'll just be a moment."

Angela appeared holding a plate wrapped in brown paper. "Two slices, still warm from the oven. You can return the plate next week. Any progress on the house hunt?"

I shook my head.

"A woman I'm acquainted with through the Ladies Aid Society is considering a move back east to be with her son. Her house might work. I'll keep my ear on it for you."

"Her ear as you've observed is the best there is."

"I heard that, Briscoe."

"Of course you did."

"Thank you so much for the pie and the ear."

"And the family?"

"Angela, for heaven sakes must you pry."

"Who's prying? I'm merely living vicariously through the young man's happiness, no thanks to you."

"Vi . . . car . . . I . . . us . . ."

"Told you, you wouldn't understand."

"You'll be the first to know," I said.

"Splendid."

"Now you are both free to resume carrying on," I said, making a hasty exit.

"See the kind of notions people jump to with you carrying on like you do, Briscoe."

"You're the one called me dear, dear."

"There you go again. You'll have my reputation in tatters."

"The Ladies Aid would never hear of it. Besides," he gave her a peck on the cheek. "You love it."

She stomped off to the kitchen, hiding a trace of pink in her cheek and biting the bud of a smile.

CHAPTER EIGHT

Sheriff's Office
Cheyenne

Late afternoon sun turned the office a tawny glow. The door opened to a young lad who ran telegrams for Western Union. Habb Tyler accepted the foolscap and tossed the boy a quarter. He slit it open and read before sliding it across his desk to Longstreet.

> *Sidney*
> *Suspects in custody–stop*
> *Holding for extradition–stop*
> *T. J. Picket, Sheriff*

Longstreet passed the telegram to young Adams.

"Slicker than snot on a doorknob."

"Suppose you could call it that. Habb, you want to collect the prisoners? It's a collar you can run for reelection on."

"If it's all the same to you, I'll stay here.

Take Seth along. Good experience for him to see firsthand how the league works."

"Fine with me. We'll catch the morning eastbound to Sidney. Should be back by evening."

Sidney
Nebraska Territory

T. J. Picket was a rail of a scarecrow a Nebraska prairie wind might blow away. They found him hunched over a rolltop desk ciphering a ledger of fines, taxes, and judgments he'd collected and his percentage due pending county board approval.

"Sheriff Picket?"

"I am. Says who?"

"Beau Longstreet, Great Western Detective League. This here's Seth Adams, Deputy Sheriff in Cheyenne. We're here to collect the prisoners you picked up."

"Pleased to meet you." Picket rose extending a bony hand. "I got 'em. Bundle of cash too. Twenty-five thousand's quite a sum. Bank payin' a reward for recovery?"

"Twenty-five hundred is the amount the directors need to approve."

"Worth the collar sure enough. McNabb can be a little surly. Keep an eye on him. The banker type is just that. Near to wet hisself when we picked him up. When you want to take custody?"

"How about after lunch in time for the westbound back to Cheyenne. If you care to join us, I'll buy."

"Best offer I had all day."

"Least we can do by way of thanks for quick work."

"Slice of that reward money be thanks aplenty."

"What's you pleasure?"

"Martha's Café, across the street in the next block. Next thing to home cookin'."

"Sounds good." And it was.

Strolling back to the jail after lunch Longstreet glanced at young Adams.

"Seth, how about you run the prisoner transfer back to Cheyenne and I'll tag along on your lead."

"If you say so, Mr. Longstreet. You have a set of shackles we can use, Sheriff?"

"Do. You can truss 'em up like a Christmas goose. Send 'em back when you finish."

"Will do." He glanced at his watch. "Would you mind doing us one more favor?"

"What do you need?"

"Wire Sheriff Tyler in Cheyenne. We won't get back until after the bank is closed. With all this cash we'll be carrying, someone from the bank probably should meet the train with a guard to take custody of it."

"Good thought."

Longstreet nodded. *Good thought.*

With the prisoners shackled, Seth took charge of a sullen McNabb, leaving Longstreet to escort a distraught Prather to the depot. Seth marched them down the platform to the last westbound passenger car. They boarded the train seating the prisoners in the second to last row of the car, McNabb at the window, Prather on the aisle. Adams took the aisle across from the prisoners, asking Longstreet to sit in the row behind them. *Knows his business for a young man,* Beau thought taking his seat. Got McNabb in a box and Prather in his way.

The westbound Union Pacific slow-rolled into Cheyenne, breaking to a screeching stop. Longstreet led Prather off the train. Seth followed McNabb, carrying a satchel bulging with the bank's cash. Sheriff Tyler waited on the platform with Charles Weston and the bank's cashier. The cashier took charge of the cash.

"I'll see this gets back to the bank," Sheriff Tyler said.

"Thank you, Sheriff," Weston said. "I'm pleased to tell you the board has authorized a recovery award in the amount of twenty-five hundred dollars."

"Much appreciated, Charles. Seth, you and Beau take these two birds over to the jail and lock 'em up. I'll see you there soon as I see the bank's money back in the vault where it belongs."

Sheriff's Office
Cheyenne

With the prisoners locked away, Beau and Seth took seats in the office to wait for Sheriff Tyler.

"So, what happens to the twenty-five-hundred-dollar reward?"

Longstreet smiled. "Best to wait for Habb to answer that question." At that the door swung open to Sheriff Tyler. "Habb, Seth here has a question for you. What happens to the reward money?"

Tyler took his barrel-back desk chair and rocked. "Let's see, the league will take a thousand. That leaves fifteen hundred for the officers. Sheriff Picket made the collar. That gets him seven-hundred fifty dollars. That leaves seven-hundred fifty dollars for this office. Beau here earned his half, three-hundred seventy-five dollars. That leaves us three-hundred seventy-five, which I figure goes to you Seth on a count a, you done most of the work."

Adams eyes bugged. His jaw dropped. "Three-hundred seventy-five dollars?"

"That's about it."

"What about you, Sheriff?"

"We coulda split it, but like I said you done most of the work. 'Sides I'll get my little piece come the league annual bonus."

"What's that?"

"Part of the league rewards and recoveries for the year get set aside for payout to all league members in equal shares at the end of the year. That way everybody pays close attention to any case the league sends their way."

"Much obliged, Sheriff. That's like six months' pay."

"S'pose it is."

Great Western Detective League Offices Denver

Beau caught the next train back to Denver. He returned to the office and made a full report to the Colonel.

Crook rocked back in his desk chair. Clasped his hands across his vest buttons and fingered the gold chain to his watch. "Splendid work, Beau. A big collar in short order."

"I had help."

"Habb Taylor?"

75

"Some, but I'm talking about his young deputy, Seth Adams. Might be one to keep your eye on."

"Why so?"

"Young, smart, well made. Took to the case quick. I had him run the prisoner extradition from Sidney. Knows his business. Thinks ahead."

"Seth Adams," Crook scratched a note on the Cattlemen's Bank case file. "Sounds like the sort we can use around here."

"You have anything pressing for me at the moment?"

"Things are a little quiet just now. If something pops up, Briscoe is here. Take a couple of days off for a job well done."

"My thanks."

Leaving Crook's office, Longstreet paused. "Briscoe, I'm taking a couple of days off. If anything comes up, you know where to find me."

Cane smiled. "Who is she this time?"

"Don't know yet."

On the boardwalk Longstreet started toward O'Rourke House.

"Hey handsome. Don't you dare run off on me like that."

The familiar voice brought him up in his tracks. He turned slowly, a smile spreading.

"Samantha."

"The very same."

Longstreet drank her vision. Blue-black hair rolled in soft coils, violet eyes, porcelain cream complexion, hourglass figure, throaty melted butter voice with an appetite for fun.

"What brings you to Denver?"

"It could be you."

"It could be. More likely some Pinkerton business for Reggie."

"You found me out." She slipped her arm in his.

"Where are you taking me?"

"You are taking me. I'm staying at the Palace. Let's have a drink and some dinner."

"Are you on a case?"

"Nine to five undercover internal fraud investigation. Very hush-hush. And you?"

"Just wrapped up a bank fraud in Cheyenne. The Colonel gave me a few days off."

"Purrr-fect timing then." She squeezed his arm.

"It would seem so."

Palace Hotel

They found a quiet table in the elegantly appointed Palace Hotel salon and ordered whiskies.

Samantha lifted her glass. "To old times."

"To good times."

"They were."

"Been awhile since the Royal Gorge dustup. As I recall you were working that with Travane. He in on this case?"

"Trev will be in on the pickup when we're ready for cuffing."

"And you decided to look up an old friend."

"Trevor is a pleasant enough diversion. There is only one Beau Longstreet."

"You'll have my head swollen."

"I'll risk it. Let's see, as long as we are reminiscing, when we made a lovely end to that case in Chicago, you were nursing a broken heart. Did you ever find out what became of the widow O'Rourke?"

"Vanished without a trace."

"Did you look?"

"Made a few inquiries. Nothing turned up."

"Probably for the better, love. You and I aren't the matrimonial sort. Though I will own if I were tempted to indulge the marital state, you'd be one hell of a catch."

"There you go again. How does a man measure up to expectations like that?"

"You know perfectly well. It's how I came by them. Now let's have some dinner before I am forced to straighten your tie."

"Is it crooked again?"

"It's always crooked, Beau Longstreet. Just before it comes off."

CHAPTER NINE

Cattlemen's Club
Cheyenne, Wyoming Territory

Ranchers Buck McGant and Davis Chesterfield sat huddled around one of the game tables with a bottle of bourbon and glasses; McGant McGant served the Wyoming Stock Growers Association as president, Chesterfield held the treasurer's post. They were joined by stock detectives Jack Black and Red "Rusty" Gates.

"Lynching sent a message for sure," McGant said. "Left us under a lot of suspicion we could just as well do without."

Chesterfield bunched his brows, "You sayin' we should ease back, Buck?"

"Not sayin' that at all. We need to run those squatters off our range. We just need to find a way to do it that don't cast the shadow of suspicion on us. You boys are professionals; what do you think, Jack?"

Black glanced at Gates who shrugged.

"We could try to do it legally."

"How?" Chesterfield said.

"Frame up rustling charges and let the courts deal with the problem."

McGant refilled his glass. "You figure you can do that with all of 'em?"

"No. Two maybe three. We put up a big policing presence. Get a conviction or two and the rest will figure it can happen to any of them. We'll make sure they come to that conclusion. Let 'em know, if they know what's good for them, they best clear out."

"What do you think, Davis?"

"Might work. What do you think, Buck?"

"Might. Ranch work can be dangerous too, Jack. Couple of 'em have an accident, adds weight to the get out message."

Black lifted his glass, "That's why you're the boss, Mr. McGant."

Pendleton Ranch
Johnson County

The Big Horns ranged a ragged purple horizon in the west drawn closer by a stiff breeze and a line of dark clouds threatening a storm. Black and Gates pushed a half-dozen head of branded cattle onto the Pendleton range, mingled with Pendleton stock.

"That should do it," Black said. "Ranch

house is over the rise yonder." They wheeled away at a lope to the ranch house.

Will Pendleton watched two riders lope up the lane to the yard. They drew rein.

"Will Pendleton?"

"I am."

"You're under arrest."

"Who says."

"Jack Black, Stock Detective, Wyoming Stock Growers Association."

"On what charge?"

"Rustling."

"Rustling? I don't know what you are talking about."

"We do. There's half a dozen brands mixed in with your little valley herd."

"I don't know anything about that. They must be strays."

"Strays don't leave a trail driving them here. Cuff him, Rusty."

Red-haired rider stepped down.

"Someone else must have driven them then. I had nothing to do with that."

Rusty cuffed his hands. "Save it for the judge."

Sherriff's Office
Buffalo

Johnson County Sheriff Ben Whitaker propped his feet up on the desk, relaxing a

82

bit at the end of a long day. Boots on the boardwalk cut his respite short. He dropped his boots to the floor as the office door swung open. Black and Gates again, this time with Wiley Turner.

"Got room for one more, Sheriff?"

"Don't tell me, let me guess, rustling."

"Easy to spot 'em once we collar 'em."

"Sheriff, I tried tellin' these jaspers I didn't rustle no stock. I got no idea how them cattle got mixed in with mine. They claim they trailed 'em, but I didn't drive 'em."

"They all say that, Sheriff. Lock 'em up."

"Take his cuffs off. Curious how Wiley's story sounds so much like Will Pendleton's. You'll still have to file a complaint."

"You do your job, Sheriff, and I'll do mine. Give me the paperwork."

"This way, Wiley."

"You got Will in here too?"

"What you lockin' Wiley up for?" Pendleton said.

"Rustlin', same as you, Will."

The cell door swung open with a creak.

"Somethin' ain't right, Sheriff. Somethin' just ain't right."

"That'll be for a judge and jury to sort out."

Shaw Ranch
Johnson County

Dan Shaw sat his horse watching as two men pushed a handful of cattle southeast toward a small herd he had pastured nearby. Having heard what happened to Will Pendleton and Wiley Turner he had a pretty good idea who and why. He drew his Winchester from its saddle boot and squeezed up a lope on a line to put himself between the drovers and his herd. He drew rein and wheeled around to face them, blocking the way with his rifle across the cantle of his saddle.

Black and Gates drew rein.

"Where do you think you are going with those cattle on my range?"

Black spoke. "We're taking 'em back where they belong, on public grassland."

"Was public. I own it now and those ain't my cows."

"They may not be your cows, but they got every right to this range."

"Not if it comes with a trumped-up rustling charge."

"Don't know what you're talkin' about."

"Will Pendleton and Wiley Turner know what I'm talkin' about." He jacked a round in the chamber of his rifle. "Now get the hell off my land."

"Ain't your land."

"Homestead Act says it is. You're trespassin'. You turn them cows around and head north. All the public range you say you're lookin' for is out there. Another step south and I'll be protecting my property rights."

"We'll see about your property rights, Shaw. You'd be well advised to pull up stakes and homestead your ass somewhere else."

"Don't think so, Black."

"See there, Rusty, Shaw here is one of them uppity ones. Powers that be don't cotton to their kind. Be seein' you, Shaw. Count on it. Come on, Rusty, let's turn 'em. For now."

League Office
Denver

Longstreet sat at his desk in lengthening shadows, pouring over a stack of wanted dodgers making the rounds of the office. The door opened to the visitor bell. Samantha scanned the room, her eyes coming to rest on Beau. She crossed the office.

"Still in town?"

"Still in town. I see you're back to the salt mine. Anything interesting?"

"Only if I spot one."

"Pity. I thought I might interest you."

He returned a dodger to the stack. "Now that you mention it."

"That's better. Quittin' time. You know what they say."

Longstreet rose. "No. What do they say?"

"All work and no play . . ."

"Don't see a Jack anywhere in sight."

"Guess you'll have to do then, handsome." She took his arm.

"Who's taking who?"

"Does it matter?"

"Where then?"

"You look like you could use a drink. Supper then and I'll venture to speculate, your tie is a fright."

"Gonna have to do something about that tie."

"I know."

"Drinks followed by steaks in the Palace dining room."

"This could be more of a regular thing if Reggie gets his way."

"Gets his way about what?"

"He's trying to convince Mr. Pinkerton to transfer me to the Denver office."

"How do you feel about that?"

She lifted a lash. "I like the view. If the money is right, I could get used to the climate. What would you think about having me in town?"

"I like the view?"

"I'm sure you do."

"You think it might happen?"

"I don't know. Mr. Pinkerton appreciates my versatility. It's disarming, you know."

"So, I've heard."

"Reggie claims he has enough work to keep me billable. It's an argument Pinkerton understands."

"Do you get a say?"

"Some. Short of saying I quit."

"And if you had to say, short of saying I quit?"

"I do like the view."

"Then, I guess, we agree."

"We are."

"What?"

"Most agreeable."

Chapter Ten

Johnson County Courthouse
Buffalo

Rain pattered the roof and streaked the windows. The packed courtroom grew warm and stuffy, smelling of wet wool and bodies ripened well past their June baths. Half the county knew what was at stake for the verdict. The curious filled the courtroom to standing room, spilling outside the door in the corridor, straining to hear the proceedings.

"The defense calls Dan Shaw to the stand."

Dan approached the bench, conscious all eyes in the courtroom were on him, not the least of which were two Wyoming Stock Growers Association detectives.

The bailiff offered the bible in his hand. "Raise your right hand. Do you solemnly swear to tell the truth, the whole truth, and nothing but the truth, so help you God?"

"I do."

"The witness may be seated. The defense may proceed."

"Now Mr. Shaw, you have heard the defendant, Mr. Pendleton, testify he had no knowledge of how cattle, not of his ownership, came into his herd. You have also heard Mr. Black and Mr. Gates testify they followed the trail of those cows being driven onto Mr. Pendleton's range. Would you now please tell the court and this jury about your recent encounter with Mr. Black and Mr. Gates on your ranch."

"I was out checking a water tank when I observed two riders driving a small herd of cattle onto my land. Knowing what happened to Will here and Wiley, I became suspicious."

"By Wiley, you mean Wiley Turner, whose rustling charges are similar to those against Mr. Pendleton, though they have yet to come before this court."

"Yes, sir."

"You may proceed."

"Your Honor, the prosecution objects! Mr. Shaw has nothing to do with the offense in question."

"Your Honor, the defense will show Mr. Shaw's testimony will establish a pattern of action by Wyoming Stock Growers Association stock detectives common to Mr. Pendleton's case and in turn that of Mr. Turner."

"Overruled. The defense may proceed."

"Now Mr. Shaw, did you act on your suspicions?"

"I did."

"And please tell the court, what transpired."

"The riders was headed toward my herd, so I rode in to stop them."

"And who were they?"

"Them two stock detectives."

"Let the record show Mr. Shaw identified Mr. Black and Mr. Gates. Then what happened?"

"The cattle were mixed brands, just like Will and Wiley's cases. I asked 'em where they were going with those cows. They said they were takin' 'em back where they belong. I told 'em they was on my land and they oughta turn 'em back north to range that was open."

"And did they?"

"Not right off. They said I was squattin' on public graze and if I knew what's good for me I'd pick up and get gone."

"They threatened you."

"You could take it that way. I had my Winchester and told 'em they was trespassin' and I'd be in my rights to protect my property."

"And did they comply?"

"They did."

"Your Honor, Mr. Black and Mr. Gates allege in their complaint they followed the trail made by the cattle being driven into Mr. Pendleton's herd. In time this court will hear a similar claim in the case of Mr. Turner."

"Objection! Irrelevant."

"Sustained. The jury will disregard reference to a matter not before this court at this time. Is the defense finished?"

"Not quite, Your Honor. In Mr. Shaw's encounter with Mr. Black and Mr. Gates they quite literally followed the trail of cattle driven onto Mr. Shaw's land. Cattle driven by Mr. Black and Mr. Gates. Is it possible then that the cattle driven into Mr. Pendleton's herd were driven by . . ."

"Objection! Mr. Black and Mr. Gates are not on trial here."

"Sustained."

"Your Honor, I don't intend to accuse Mr. Black or Mr. Gates personally, if I may finish?"

"Proceed, but be careful."

"Is it possible then that the cattle driven into Mr. Pendleton's herd were driven by someone other than Mr. Pendleton? Your witness."

Denver Tribune

Outlawry and Corruption Reign
in Johnson County

Cheyenne Leader *reports rancher Will Pendleton acquitted of open and shut rustling charges by a jury of Johnson County peers. Case against Wiley Turner dismissed. Wyoming Stock Growers Association President Buck McGant outraged. "Buffalo is run by rustlers. Honest ranchers are being run off public land by thievery while the law looks the other way. Something must be done."*

Longstreet handed the paper to Cane.

"The big boys won't be happy about this."

"Big boys?"

"Big ranchers. Cattle barons make up the Wyoming Cattle Growers Association. Small ranchers and farmers settled in Johnson County under the Homestead Act on land that was once open range. Public grassland the big ranchers use to pasture some of their herds. They got no use for the homesteaders. The way they figure it small operators and homesteaders are squatting on their land."

"The law's the law."

"We see it that way, but Washington law is a long way from Wyoming. I heard some of it in the Cattlemen's Club in Cheyenne while I was up there on that bank fraud case."

"You figure they'll have trouble?"

"Wouldn't be the first range war started over a grazing rights dispute."

"Rustlin's still a crime."

"It is. Then again, there's a judge and jury up there don't think either one of those boys are rustlers."

"Paper makes it sound like the whole county's corrupt."

"Not surprising."

"How so?"

"*Cheyenne Leader* is owned by big cattle money."

O'Rourke House
1911

A shaft of late afternoon golden light followed Angela through the leaded glass and lace-curtained front door. Cane looked up from his newspaper.

"How was the Ladies Aid?"

She tugged the bonnet ribbon bow at her chin. "Having trouble deciding who to aid."

"That's a problem if you're an aid society. Have a seat and I'll pour us a drink."

"Supper won't make itself."

"Take a sniff."

"Bacon?"

"Flapjacks and biscuits with your peach preserves."

"Breakfast for supper?"

"No law against it I know of."

"You cooked?"

"Ain't illegal either. Lady of the house deserves an evening at leisure."

"That's so sweet. I don't know what to say."

"Three fingers or two."

She smiled "Two will do. You know the rules."

"Two's good. Leaves room for a second."

"You're incorrigible."

"Thought I was sweet. Encourage-able too."

"You're impossible." She took her place on the settee and watched him pour two glasses at the dining room sideboard. He handed her a glass and took a seat beside her.

"To us," he said.

"What us?"

"Three years today I took a room here. Sort of an anniversary."

"I suppose. Well thank you for preparing breakfast." She touched the rim of her glass to his and took a swallow. "There is one bit of news from my meeting. Ethel David has decided to move back east with her son. Her house is going up for sale. It's the one I spoke to Robert about. I asked her to let he and Penny have first look. She agreed as long as they do it quickly. She is anxious to get on with her plan. Will Robert be along tomorrow?"

"Saturday, isn't it, and by the look of that bottle we shall be in need of further remuneration."

"Pity it's gone."

"Not gone. Four fingers left. Two for each of us."

"Are you plying me with strong spirits?"

"Are you encourage-able?"

"It's you who are incorrigible."

"And here all this time I thought I was sweet."

"It happens. I just don't see you making a habit of it."

"Making breakfast for supper? I don't see that habit forming."

"See what I mean? You're impossible."

"Impossibly sweet. I like the sound of that. Is that a promotion from 'dear'?"

"Don't tempt me."

"Another two fingers?"

"Fortification for facing your breakfast for supper."

"That's my girl."

"I'm not your girl."

"Have to be."

"I see no such obligation."

"I guess you missed it."

"Missed what?"

"I got no other girl."

"Pour me that drink."

CHAPTER ELEVEN

O'Rourke House
1911

Angela answered my knock at the door.

"Robert, come in, come in."

The foyer smelled of floor wax with fresh baked bread wafting from the kitchen.

"I have news for you."

"News for me?"

"Yesterday at the Ladies Aid I spoke with Ethel David. She is putting her house up for sale to move back east with her son. I thought of you and Penny. She is happy for you to have the first look at it, as long as you do so promptly."

"Where is it located?"

"15 Aspen Lane."

"I know Aspen Lane. It is on the way home from here. I'll stop on my way home this afternoon and arrange an appointment to see it."

"Splendid. I do hope something comes of

it for both of you. Briscoe, Robert is here!"

"Coming." The stairs gave out a creak underfoot.

He led the way into the parlor. We took seats.

"So, where were we?"

Cattlemen's Club

McGant fumed. Black and Gates wanted no part of the boss in a foul mood.

"What's to be done? That's the question." McGant said more to himself than in expectation of a response. "The courts are a waste of time. Professional help. That's what has to be done."

"Professional help?" Black ventured.

"Let me worry about that. For now, you two get back up to that rat's nest. Keep the pressure on. Do whatever you have to do. I don't want to know what you're up to; but damn it, I want results. Start with Shaw. He knows too much, and from what you told me, he was the hero of the Pendleton trial. Make an example of him. Maybe some others will get the message."

Shaw Ranch
Johnson County

Black and Gates drew rein in a willow-break upstream from the Shaw homestead. Black fixed a glass on the buildings and yard. The layout consisted of a small cabin and barn with a corral. Wash on a line beside the cabin said the wife was likely home. He saw no sign of the husband.

"Looks pretty quiet, Rusty. Laundry on the line says ladies' work. No sign of Shaw. Let's ride on in. Spook her enough maybe he takes the hint."

Black squeezed up a lope, Gates tucked in at his stirrup.

Riders comin'. Susan felt alone. She propped a shotgun just inside the open cabin door.

The riders drew rein.

"Mrs. Shaw?"

"Who's askin'?"

"Jack Black, this here's Rusty Gates. We're Wyoming Cattle Growers Association stock detectives."

"I know who you are."

"Your husband about?"

"I expect him directly. What do you want with Dan?"

"You folks is squatted on open range here. You need to clear out."

"We've a legal right to homestead here."

"Washington law is a long way from Wyoming. Don't draw no water here."

"Then all you need to do is get a court to

agree with you."

"Sassy too, ain't she, Rusty? Ain't wastin' no time on Johnson County kangaroo courts. Now mark my words, you and your husband know what's good for you, you'll pack up and be on your way."

"Is that a threat?"

"Take it however you like. Your husband already pissed off powerful people the way he testified for Pendleton. If I were him, I'd be right careful. You tell him I said so."

"Tell him yourself. Here he comes now."

Returning home with a mule deer strapped over the back of his saddle, Dan saw two mounted men in the yard talking to Susan. Recognizing the horses, he lifted the hammer thong on his Colt and spurred up a gallop home.

Black and Gates turned to meet him.

Dan pulled up and stepped down.

"You alright, dear?"

"Glad you're here."

"What do you two want?"

"Simple. I'm orderin' you off our range."

"Ain't your range anymore. You're trespassin' on my land again."

"Rustlers got no land rights in Wyoming."

"We ain't never rustled nothing. This here land is available to settle by the Homestead Act."

"This here's Wyoming Territory. Like we told your wife Washington law is a long way from here."

"We're here lawfully."

"The hell you say. I say you're a rustler squattin' on public grazing land and I'm orderin' you off it."

"On who's authority?"

"Wyoming Stock Growers Association, that's who."

Dan spit. "The same growers who make a practice of lynchin' innocent folks? The same growers who make trumped-up rustling charges that don't stand up in court? Now get your sorry asses off my land."

Black drew his gun. "You're in no position to order anybody off public grazing land. Resist our order and you should expect to suffer the fate any rustler caught in the act deserves. Do I make myself clear?"

Click, click, sounded behind Black and Gates. Susan stood resolute in the cabin doorway, a double-barreled shotgun leveled at the two stock detectives.

"Now put that thing away, little lady, before you and your rustling husband get hurt."

Click. Dan leveled his Colt at Black and Gates. "Now drop those guns and ride out of here before I shoot you for trespassin'."

Black and Gates dropped their guns. "This ain't over, Shaw. Not by a long shot. Hear that? Long shot. I'd watch my back if I was you."

"If I was a bushwhacker like you, it'd have to be a back shoot. Now get!"

15 Aspen Lane
Denver
1911

We walked from the apartment Sunday afternoon. The moment I saw the place Saturday after leaving Briscoe, I knew Penny would love it. A neatly whitewashed clapboard on a quiet tree-lined side street. Flower beds across the front of the house flanking a comfortable front porch complete with a swing. Penny took it all in.

"Oh, Robert. It looks, it looks perfect."

"We haven't seen the inside yet."

"Can we afford it?"

"We'll soon find out."

"Oh, look there! The flower beds. Columbine, the flowers of our wedding bouquets. It's a sign. It's meant to be."

I put my arm around her with a let's-not-get-ahead-of-ourselves look I had no conviction to back up. I love her so hard it hurts when she glows like that. I rapped on the door.

Mrs. David greeted us.

"Mrs. David, may I present my wife, Penny."

"Pleasure to meet you, Mrs. David."

"And you, dear. Please call me Ethel. Mr. David has been gone so long I scarcely feel Mrs. anymore. Come right in. Let me show you around."

It reminded me of a smaller version of O'Rourke House. Parlor, dining room, and kitchen on the first floor. She led up a center staircase to a second-floor landing. A generous bedroom on one side, two smaller bedrooms on the other. Inspecting the nearer of the two, Penny turned misty-eyed to me.

"How perfect for a nursery."

"We raised our son in that room," Ethel said wistfully.

She led us back downstairs. "Let's have a cup of tea, shall we? Have a seat in the parlor. I've just made a fresh pot. I'll be but a moment."

"Oh, Robert, I love it. I do hope we can afford it."

"I do too, but we mustn't get our hopes up ahead of ourselves."

"But it would be ever so perfect."

"We had many the happy year here," Ethel said returning with a tea service. She handed each of us a dainty china cup and took her seat. "So, tell me. What do you think?"

"You've a lovely home here. We love it. How much will you ask?"

"I'm hoping for eleven hundred dollars."

Penny's shoulders drooped ever so slightly. I was afraid of that.

"Much as we love your home, I'm afraid it's beyond what we can afford."

"How much is that?"

"How much is what?"

"The amount you can afford to pay."

"We've saved six hundred dollars."

Ethel pursed her lips and sipped her tea. She glanced around the room. "You know when Mr. David and I built this house, we were about your age." She smiled a far-off smile. "Didn't have a stick of furniture that wasn't secondhand. Took us years to grow into this home. Good years. I'll wager you've those years ahead of you. If you were to take on a monthly payment, how much might you afford?"

I thought about my salary at the *Tribune,* book royalties erratic, a surprise every time a check came. "Reliably, twenty-five dollars a month."

She drummed her fingertips reflectively on the side of her chin. "That might be made to work."

"What might be made to work?"

"Well you see all this." She swept her arms around the room. "The furnishings. I can't take them with me. I was planning an estate sale. I'm told it might fetch two-hundred dollars. That makes eight-hundred dollars. At twenty-five dollars a month for three years, I come out with seventeen-hundred dollars and you'd have your house."

"You'd do that for us?" Penny said.

"I would. I love this house. It holds the memories of a lifetime for me. It would please me no end to know a nice young couple like Mr. David and me were making their lifetime of memories here."

With that, we all hugged.

CHAPTER TWELVE

Buffalo

The buckboard drew up at the picket fence fronting Maddie's house on Hart Street beneath a canopy of dark felt cloud. Susan Shaw stepped down, setting the tie-down to hold the buckskin mule. She swung through the gate's distinctive chirp for the short walk to a door that swung open before her knock.

Maddie O'Rourke greeted her guest with a warm smile. "Susan, what a pleasant surprise."

"I wish it were."

"Trouble?"

Susan's eyes welled up as she nodded.

"Come in. I've just made a fresh pot of tea." Maddie held the door leading to a small, comfortably appointed parlor. "Have a seat. I'll just be a moment with the tea."

Susan took a seat to the rattle of dishes across the foyer in the kitchen. Maddie emerged with two steaming cups. She set them on a low table fronting the settee and took her place beside Susan.

"Now tell me what troubles you so."

"We had a visit from two Wyoming Stock Growers Association detectives. They accused Dan of rustling and ordered us off what they said is public grazing land."

"It may have been once, but that was before the Homestead Act."

"They claim some eastern law doesn't apply in Wyoming."

"But it does."

"Don't mean the cattle barons mean to abide it." Tears trickled down her cheeks. "Worst of all, they threatened to kill Dan for the way he testified for Will Pendleton. I'm so scared Miss Maddie, I don't know what to do."

Maddie put her arm around the girl. "There, there. Have you spoken to Sheriff Whitaker?"

Susan sniffed. "He says every small rancher in Johnson County has seen or heard the same or similar threats. Threats ain't a crime and he can't protect all of us all the time. What are we to do?"

Maddie let her gaze drift beyond lace-curtained windows. "We'll think of something. We'll think of some way to help. We'll thing of . . ." *Someone. Someone who could help. Why would he? He would. She knew he would. He'd come with a risk. Could she bear it? Did she have real courage to her convictions? Maybe he'd come to see she had the right of it. Maybe. Yet in her heart of hearts she wasn't so sure.*

She patted Susan's hand. "Leave it to me. Until then, be careful."

Maddie watched Susan pick up the tie-down and climb onto the buckboard seat. *Beau.* She took herself back to the settee. She set her mind adrift. She'd managed to live behind the fortress of her rules for a time. Her mind's eye filled with her sense of him. Slowly he'd worn her defenses away. She remembered the evening it all . . .

They passed a pleasant supper at Del-monico's from wine to cherry pie for dessert. The walk home was pleasant too, aglow with moderation. Maddie let them in the front door.

"Would you care for a cup of coffee?"

"I would."

She lit a lamp in the parlor and took herself off to the kitchen, leaving Beau to his thoughts. He took a seat on the settee.

She carried two steaming cups of coffee into the parlor and set them on the table before it and took a seat. She picked up a cup and blew gently over the steaming surface and took a small sip.

"Pleasant end to a lovely evening. I must say I haven't enjoyed myself that much in a long time."

"Now there's a pity. Life has so much to offer if you only give it the chance."

"Yes, I suppose that's true. It's only that after Matthew passed away, I haven't had much reason to give it the chance."

"Perhaps you should think about giving it a try."

She arched a brow. "Waxing philosophical or volunteering, are we?"

"Sorry, none of my business really." He retreated to his coffee cup.

"Don't be sorry, Beau. I didn't mean that the way it sounded. You pushed me out of my nest. I had a wonderful time. It just made me a little uncomfortable."

"Good."

"Why is that good?"

"Because you had a wonderful time. Interesting, really."

"How so?"

"While you were making the coffee, I was thinking that I had a wonderful time because you made me feel comfortable. Now you say you had a wonderful time and it made you uncomfortable."

"There you go with that silver-tongued blarney again. You can't fool me, Beau Longstreet. I know your kind."

"You doubt my sincerity? I am cut to the quick."

"Don't be silly." She gathered up the cups and took them to the kitchen.

He stood waiting at the foot of the stairs to his room. She paused as she passed on the way to the back of the house.

"I did have a wonderful time."

He lifted her chin, her eyes green liquid in the dim light of the parlor lamp. He kissed her ever so softly.

"I too had a wonderful time, no blarney about it."

She returned his kiss.

"Now you've made me uncomfortable. I'll turn out the lamp. You run along before I'm accused of undue fraternization."

She remembered feeling his eyes on her as she made her way down the hall to her room. She remembered enjoying the feeling as he huffed out the lamp.

Beau Longstreet. What if he comes? What if he doesn't? He'll come. Then what?

League Office
Denver

Crook flipped through the day's mail stack. *Hmm, one for Longstreet addressed in feminine hand. What has he got himself up to*

110

now? He left his office, found Longstreet at his desk. He laid the letter on the desk. "Mail call."

Beau glanced at it. *Buffalo, Wyoming Territory,* familiar hand. He tore it open.

Buffalo, Wyoming Territory

Dearest Beau,
I take pen in hand torn at cross purposes between better judgment and need. That I write, need is the greater purpose. I write to ask for help I do not deserve in a matter akin to those over which my fears denied us our happiness. It is a matter of life and death, though my life is in no danger, at this time. I shall briefly explain.

On moving to Buffalo I made a small investment in a ranching enterprise as part of my livelihood. The ranch is owned, with my invested assistance, by a young couple, Dan and Susan Shaw, who work very hard to make their homestead a success. Their ranch and others like it here in Johnson County are resented by large ranching interests, principally those in Cheyenne. The cattle barons have banded together to form a stock growers association which, among other things, seeks to run small ranchers and homesteaders off

111

lands the association deems public grazing. The cattle barons are on the wrong side of rights conferred under the Homestead Act. but they are powerful. They have sought redress in the courts with unfounded rustling charges. When the courts ruled in favor of the accused, it appears the stock growers resolved to take matters into their own hands. Of late they have resorted to threats of violence local law enforcement is powerless to resist.

The Shaws are in peril. I could think of no way to help them, other than appealing to a man of your unique abilities. If, all things considered, you determine this is not your fight, I shall understand. At least for now, in this letter, I shall take hope.

Love,
Maddie

Longstreet let the letter drop to his lap. Seth Adams's warning — "Watch" — caught cold in his breast. Maddie. *Love, Maddie.*

"Trouble?" Crook said.

"Maddie . . . Maddie's in trouble. Colonel, I need some time off. I've got to go to her."

"What kind of trouble?"

"Heard some about it around the Cattlemen's Club in Cheyenne. Smells like range war brewing between Wyoming Stock Growers Association members and small ranchers up in Johnson County. Maddie's managed to get herself mixed up on the small ranchers' side of the dustup. Those Cheyenne boys play rough. Lynching, rustling charges, now murder threats."

"How long will you be gone?"

Beau shrugged. "No idea."

"Alright, you do what you have to do. One minute though." Crook turned his head over his shoulder. "Briscoe, can you come over here a minute."

Cane left his desk.

"Beau, you can't take on this bunch without somebody havin' your back."

"Ain't Briscoe's fight."

"Isn't your fight either."

Cane gave a puzzled look. "What fight?"

Longstreet handed Cane the letter.

"Beau here is hell-bent on protecting his couldn't-marry-him-for-the-danger-in-his-line-of-work damsel in distress. He shouldn't be taking on this bunch alone."

"Uh-huh," Cane muttered finishing the letter. "I take his back. That even things up?"

"We're on the morning train to Cheyenne."

Palace Hotel

Longstreet waited in the lobby, not looking

forward to this next conversation. He didn't know what to make of the situation. No idea where things were headed. There were no strings involved, other than a plan to have dinner and one thing or another. That one thing or another part made things . . . awkward.

"Hi, handsome."

"We need to talk. Let's have a drink."

"That sounds ominous. Something wrong?"

"I have to leave."

"New case?"

"Drink first."

He led her to a corner table in the salon. He ordered whiskies on the way past the bar. The bartender delivered glasses and a bottle to the table. Longstreet poured.

"It's not a case, is it?"

"Not exactly."

"It's Maddie O'Rourke, isn't it?"

"How do you know that?"

"I'm a detective. Oh, and a woman too, though I suspect you've noticed that part. She in trouble?"

"She is."

"What kind of trouble?"

"Might end up in the middle of a range war."

"Johnson County?"

"How do you know that?"

"I read the papers. Must be on the side of the small ranchers."

"And how is it you know that?"

"If she was on the side of the big boys, she wouldn't be in trouble."

"You're . . ."

"Samantha."

"I know."

"So, Maddie O'Rourke drops back into your life out of nowhere and Beau Longstreet dons his shining armor, mounts his dashing charger, and rides off to the rescue. Assuming for the moment you don't get yourself killed, where does that leave you?"

Samantha held his eyes.

"You don't know, do you? I'll tell you where. You still love her. Plain as day. All you know is she's in trouble. Is that going to change her feelings? What if it doesn't? What if in the end you end up right back where you are now, only with your heart broken again?"

"No worse off than I am now."

"Unless you get yourself killed, love. Unless you get yourself killed."

O'Rourke House
Denver
1911

I swear Angela must have been waiting at the door for my knock; it opened so quickly.

"Robert, so good to see you. How did it go with Ethel? Did you like the house?"

"The house is perfect. Mrs. David was so generous in helping us work out an arrangement by which we can afford it. She is having her lawyer draw up the sales agreement. We can move in as soon as she completes her estate sale and is ready to leave. We owe you a great debt of gratitude for steering us to her."

"Oh, Robert, that is wonderful news. I am so pleased it worked out for both of you."

"Big news is it?" Briscoe descended the stairs.

"Robert and Penny have bought Ethel David's place, dear."

"Welcome to home ownership, Robert. I prefer renting myself."

"That way, he's only in the way when it comes to doing things. Pay him no mind."

"I do things."

"Name one."

"I'm supportive and I dry dishes too. There, that's two things I do."

"Next you'll be wanting a reduction in

116

your rent."

"I've asked no such thing, though now that you mention it."

"Don't even think about it. You see what I put up with, Robert?"

"What would you two do without each other?"

"Die of peace and quiet," Angela said.

"Die of boredom more likely. You know I'm indispensable."

"That'll be the day."

"It will. Come along, Robert. Where were we?"

CHAPTER THIRTEEN

Union Pacific
Denver Spur

The Cheyenne train rolled out of Denver station the next morning promptly at seven o'clock. Cane dozed in the window seat across the aisle, leaving Longstreet alone with his thoughts. Two years since she disappeared, creating a void in his life he could never have imagined before Maddie O'Rourke. He remembered. The first time he laid eyes on her.

The Colonel's reference to "Widow O'Rourke's" boarding house conjured up a rather different expectation to the vision that greeted him at the door.

"Yes?"

"I, ah, I'm told I might find a Mrs. O'Rourke here."

"You've found her. I'm Madeline O'Rourke. And you, sir?"

"Beau, Beauregard Longstreet. Colonel

Crook suggested I might find rooming accommodations here."

She eyed him up and down.

He returned the favor. Madeline O'Rourke presented a fine figure of a woman, with wholesome good looks, waves of velvet auburn hair, and a flawless complexion splashed lightly across the bridge of an upturned nose with girlish golden freckles.

"Won't you come in, Mr. Longstreet?"

She spoke the buttery brogue of her immigrant heritage. Longstreet imagined he noticed a mischievous twinkle at the back of her dark green eyes. She stepped aside to let him in. The entry foyer floor and the hallway beyond shone off the smell of fresh wax. A scent of fresh baked bread hung in the air.

"Come this way." She led him into a comfortably appointed parlor and showed him to the settee. "Please have a seat." She took the facing wing chair.

"Have you a room for me, ma'am?"

She knit her brow. "We shall see. I must tell you I am particular about my tenants. I have a reputation to protect and I'm not yet persuaded you would be good for that."

"Was it something I said?"

"Not yet, it's just a feeling I have. Now tell me something of yourself, Mr. Longstreet. You're from the south, I take it. Where are

119

you from? What brings you to Denver?"

"My family roots are in South Carolina. I came west after the war. For the past few years, I've been employed by the Pinkerton Detective Agency. I've only this morning decided to accept a position with Colonel Crook's Great Western Detective League."

"So, you are a man of the law, then."

"Yes, ma'am."

She winced.

"What sort of work will you do for Colonel Crook?"

"I expect to take field assignments."

"So, you'll travel then."

"Yes." No ma'am, no wince.

"Your residence here would be a place to hang your hat between assignments."

He nodded.

"I suppose that might work, provided of course you agree to abide by the rules."

"Rules?"

"My house rules. Breakfast is served at seven, dinner at six-thirty. No female guests beyond the parlor. No gambling or late-night carousing on the premises. Strong drink is permitted only in moderation and I am the sole judge of moderation."

"There's a mercy."

"I beg your pardon?"

"An Irish lass in charge of moderation where

liquor is imbibed."

She flushed, caught a merry chuckle in her throat, and fixed him with a cool green reprimand. "I am indeed that judge. And to be perfectly clear on the point, I have a strict policy against fraternizing with my tenants. Is that understood?"

"Yes, ma'am."

She scowled. "If you'll come this way, I'll show you the room I have available." She led the way to a broad staircase climbing out of the foyer. "It's on the third floor, I'm afraid. I hope that's not too inconvenient."

"No, ma'am." She plainly didn't appreciate him calling her that. He smiled. It might break the ice. He followed her hips up the stairs. No fraternization indeed, rules were made to be broken.

The room was large and airy with windows on two sides. The furnishings were comfortably simple with a small writing desk, a wing chair, armoire, washbasin, and bed.

"The rent is twenty dollars a month with one month on deposit in advance. Is that acceptable?"

"Yes, ma'am."

"Oh please, Mr. Longstreet, if you are going to live here, I simply can't abide you calling me that. It feels like a dried-up old husk. My friends call me Maddie."

"Very well then, Maddie, you must call me Beau." He topped it off with a charming southern smile.

Her cheeks colored. "Very well then, Beau."

And so, it began. Gradually her feelings toward him warmed. Affection deepened to a realization of love he'd never experienced before. It progressed to the precipice of marriage. A step she couldn't take. She disappeared. For two years he knew in his heart she was missing. He knew he'd bring her back if he could. Now the possibility seemed clouded. Clouded by a veil of desperation. Fear took her away following the horror of her abduction. Fear drove her back into his life. Could two years bury the horror? What might he mean to her now? He reached in his coat pocket and drew out a letter tattered in pain.

My Dearest Beau,
It is with heartfelt pain and sorrow that I put this pen to paper. I cannot bear the thought of losing you for a decision I cannot escape. For all that I love you, and I do, I cannot be your wife. The thought of what you do and the risks you take would haunt my every waking hour for whatever life we might have together. I know you have said you would give it up and find

some other pursuit, but I cannot persuade myself such would be fair to you. I love the man you are. I shall cling to that memory always. I shall not change it. These weeks in your absence have accorded me time for clear headed thinking. I've been widowed some years now. It's not the end of the world, but I shouldn't wish to endure such loss again. I know life comes with risk. In this, my love, I'll not tempt the fates. I've sold the house to Mrs. Fitzwalter at a fair price with her assurance you are welcome to continue living there. Proceeds of the sale will allow me to reestablish myself and resume those rules that served me so well for so many years. You did make a mockery of them and I shall love you forever for it.

Maddie

Where to now, Maddie? Where to now? The front range scrolled by as the U.P. ran north. Beau let his mind drift to pleasant memories. He recalled slowly dismantling the carefully constructed defenses surrounding her heart. Something about her he'd found irresistible. She resisted him alright. Vexed him that she did. Beau Longstreet wasn't used to being resisted. That Beau Longstreet might have moved on to easier pursuits. He didn't. Time passed. Comfort set in. Comfort deepened to something more. Something new to his experience. First love. She opened her heart to the realization and let him in, only to have evil intrude on their bliss. He could still taste the fear he felt when she went missing. The relief when they won her release. The total loss he felt in her letter. Two years. Two years dulled the hurt. Now another letter and in his heart, nothing had changed. What of her? What of Maddie? Where to now?

Cheyenne

The Denver train slow-rolled along Sixteenth Street into the depot. Longstreet and Cane gathered their belongings and headed down the swaying aisle to the back of the car. The train ground to a halt to the clank of couplings. Longstreet stepped down to the platform, greeted by a hot gust of Wyoming hospitality. He led the way back to the stock car. They waited while stockmen rolled a ramp in place, unloading Smoke first, followed by Yankee. Both would need a little time to recover their land legs. They led the horses east on Sixteenth to Rawlins House at the corner of Sixteenth and Dodge Street. They stabled the horses in the hotel stable before checking in.

"Stowe your gear and meet me back here," Longstreet said.

"Where we off to?"

"Sherriff's office. We'll see if he has any sense of the situation up north. We'll need supplies and a packhorse. We can pick up a pack animal at the livery and then make a stop at the general store."

Sheriff's Office

Deputy Seth Adams was on duty when Longstreet and Cane came calling.

"Mr. Longstreet, what brings you back to Cheyenne?"

"Trouble up north, Seth. Meet my partner, Briscoe Cane. Briscoe, Seth Adams."

Cane and Adams exchanged hands.

"Seth is the young man I told you and the Colonel about. He was a big help on that bank fraud case."

"I don't know about help, Mr. Longstreet. I for sure learned a lot for the experience."

"Don't sell yourself short, Seth. Enough folks willing to do that for most of us, there's no need for us to pitch in. By the way, you best call me Beau. We're in this law business together now. What can you tell us about the situation in Johnson County?"

125

"Not much has changed since you and I last spoke of it. The big ranchers are dead set on keeping public land public. The Stock Growers Association been hirin' stock detectives aplenty. Seem to prefer the rough sort handy with a gun."

"How many?"

"Hard to say. Couple dozen at least. The barons isn't given to reporting their doin's to us."

"Have there been any murders?"

"Not since the suspect hangin's you know about. Leastwise, I haven't heard of any. What sort of trouble got you up here?"

"A friend sent for us. Seems some of the ranchers have been threatened."

"Not surprising. Like I said, them big boys is dead set on keepin' the open range open."

"We need supplies and a packhorse," Cane said.

"Mercantile is two doors down. I'd start there before they close. Livery is east end of town. I'd let you bunk in the jail, except I got a full house just now. Rawlins House is two blocks east."

"Thanks for the offer of the jail, we're already checked in at Rawlins House. Beau, you see to the supplies while I rent us a packhorse. We'll meet back at the hotel."

"How about you bring the packhorse to

the mercantile so I don't have to pack the supplies to the hotel?"

"Always thinkin' ahead."

"Keeps us both out of trouble. How long will it take to reach Buffalo, Seth?"

Seth rubbed his chin, "Take the U.P. north to Casper, five days from there, four if you push."

"We push. Care to join us for supper?"

"I'm on duty. I'll pass the invite along to Sheriff Tyler."

Rawlins House

The dining room was quiet in early evening. Longstreet and Cane sat at a corner table with Sheriff Habb Tyler. The only other diners occupied two tables across the room.

Longstreet forked a bite of steak. "Who runs the Stock Growers Association, Habb?"

"Buck McGant and Davis Chesterfield probably carry the most weight. McGant currently serves as president if I recollect rightly. Chesterfield holds the purse strings. You may recall him being close to the bank from the fraud case."

"I do. Charles Weston persuaded him to sell me his ranch on paper to see what Prather would do to the loan application."

"I remember that now."

"Those boys go to trial yet?"

127

"Not yet. Circuit judge is due anytime now."

"Seth tells us the stock growers are hiring stock detectives cut on the rough side. Any idea how many?"

"Afraid not. Rumor is all we hear. This friend you're lookin' to help out, what's his angle?"

"Not his, her. Maddie O'Rourke moved to Buffalo two years ago. Made an investment in a small ranch, owned by a couple named Shaw. Maddie's worried they might be in danger."

"Shaw, that wouldn't be Dan Shaw, would it?"

"I believe that's the name she mentioned in her letter. Why?"

"Danger indeed. His testimony blew up rustling charges the association brought against a small rancher in a recent court case."

"Read about that in the Denver papers. If the big boys plan to play rough, that would sure make him a target."

"What do you figure to do about it?"

"Not sure. It'd help if we knew something more of what the cattle barons are planning to do with all those stock detectives. Briscoe and I probably pass for competent men. Where do we find this McGant?"

128

"McGant's southern headquarters is north of town on the way to Buffalo."

"Right handy that way," Cane said.

"Southern headquarters?"

"Big operator. He's got a northern ranch they call T.A. Ranch in southern Johnson County."

"Smack in the middle of it all."

"You could say."

Bar M Ranch

McGant's Bar M Ranch set at the south end of the Wyoming basin north of Cheyenne. Headquarters sprawled along the side of a small rise to a rambling ranch house perched atop the crest of the hill, overlooking bunkhouse, stable, and corrals.

"Big place," Cane said. Smoke agreed with a stomp.

"Is," Longstreet said.

"How you plan to play this?"

"Stock detectives lookin' for work."

"That simple."

"You got another thought?"

"Let's get to it."

They squeezed a trot up the ranch road. Passing a ranch hand in the stable yard, they drew rein.

"Where do we find Mr. McGant?" Longstreet said.

"Up to the big house."

"Much obliged."

They loped up the hill and stepped down. An imposing figure of a man stepped onto a broad porch fronting the house.

"Mr. McGant?" Longstreet asked.

"I am."

"Beau Longstreet, this here's Briscoe Cane. We understand the Stock Growers Association is hiring stock detectives."

"We are. Hiring's done in Johnson County. Lead detective up there is Jack Black. You'll find him in Buffalo."

"Mind if I ask what the association is up against."

"Damn rustlers infest the place. Squatters is invading open range. Need 'em out, root and branch."

"What about the law?"

"What law? Sheriff's one of 'em. Courts is no better. Sometimes private law is all the law you get. You competent and suited to that situation, Jack can use you. If you can't abide taking matters into your own hands, it's not a job for you."

"We'll find Jack. Thanks for your help."

"Good day then."

CHAPTER FOURTEEN

Wyoming Basin

They pushed hard after leaving U. P. Station in Casper, riding into the night when conditions afforded enough light. Two days turned to three. On the fourth day a storm blew out the Little Big Horn mountains in the west, slowing their pace to muddy and miserable. They found a sheltered outcropping up a rocky draw with enough dry fuel for a small fire. They picketed and grained the horses. Cane put on a pot of coffee to go with fatback, beans, and biscuits for their first hot meal since leaving Cheyenne. They sat around the fire after supper watching rain spatter the draw in jagged flashes of lightning and peels of thunder. At length Longstreet broke the silence.

"I been thinkin'."

"Good. My ass is too sore for it."

"Desk ridin' will do that."

"Yeah, yeah. What's on your mind?"

131

"We should make Buffalo tomorrow. Before we hit town, we split up. That way we can work both sides of the street."

"I'm listening."

"I'll go into town first and go to the livery. I'll put Yankee up there and rent a rig of some kind. As soon as I find out where Maddie lives, I'll leave a note tucked under my saddle blanket. I'll have her show me out to the Shaw place to get a handle on the situation there. Give me a couple of hours before you ride into town. See what you can do about finding Black and getting yourself hired on to stock detective work. That way we'll know what they're planning and how to deal with situations as they develop. Ride out to Maddie's place after dark so we can compare notes and figure out how to play it from there."

"Sounds like a good start. Do you think we should let the sheriff know we're in town? Usually do for league work."

"Not this time. McGant said the sheriff is one of them, making it sound like the law favors the small ranchers. He may be a stand-up guy, but until we figure out who's on what side, the fewer people know what we're up to the better."

"Makes sense." Cane squinted beyond the circle of firelight. "None of my business, other than we been together a long time. You think there's any more to this than a call for help?"

"You mean Maddie?"

"Do."

"Wish I knew, Briscoe. I've sure given it some thought all the way here."

"Know you have. I can smell smoke."

They chuckled.

"Won't know until I know."

"Best not get ahead of yourself."

Longstreet lifted a sidelong glance at saddle leather features stitched in concern and firelight. "Good advice, my friend. Thank you."

"Best turn in. I feel a hard day's ride comin' on."

Cane rolled up in his blanket. Beau settled his head on his saddle. *Any more than a call for help?* Things developed slowly between them over the course of his comings and goings. *Comings and goings.*

"It's only the wayward traveler."

She poked her head out of the kitchen. "Wayward, now there's a truer word ever spoken."

"You did miss me."

"Don't be too sure."

"Wouldn't dream of it."

"And I suppose you've missed your supper

as well," she said, glancing at the clock.

He raised his hands in mock surrender. "I know, I know. I've missed the appointed hour."

"Can't have a resident fainting from hunger; 'twould be unseemly. We've a pot roast. I can fix you a cold sandwich slice."

"Ah, Maddie dear, you're an angel of mercy."

"Don't interpret my kindness for endearment."

"Heaven forfend."

"Have a seat. I'll only be a minute."

He pulled out his usual chair next to hers at the head of the table. By the time she came from the kitchen carrying his plate he was seated with a bottle of sherry on the table.

"What's that?"

"Sherry. I brought it to celebrate my return home. I know your policy as regards strong spirits, but I thought you might make a small exception for so cultured a libation on so special an occasion."

"Special, we are now?"

"If you say so."

She feigned a frown. Opened a cupboard at the sideboard and produced two crystal glasses. Beau poured. He lifted his glass.

"To small exceptions."

"You are that."

He touched her glass. She took a sip and smiled in spite of herself.

"So, did you find your diamonds in San Francisco?"

He shook his head around a mouthful of roast beef. "No, but we think we may have a connection to the gang that was behind that bond forgery case last year."

"Really? They must be quite industrious."

"Quite. Any news about here?"

"The usual."

"Good. Then no erstwhile suitors have come along in my absence."

Piqued. "What earthly business would such a thing be of yours?"

"Just looking after my interests. Here . . . let me top that up for you." He poured. He noticed she let him.

"Your interests, is it? Your interests run to skirts. I suspect you had a woman waiting in every depot stop betwixt Cheyenne and San Francisco."

"You wound me. Though I do enjoy the wee hint of jealousy. A little green goes nicely with your eyes."

"You are impossible, Beau Longstreet."

He wiped a last bit of gravy from his lips on his napkin. "I assure you I am eminently possible."

She gathered his plate.

"Shall we take our sherry to the parlor?"

She paused at the kitchen door. "I don't

know that I'm comfortable with that."

"I am." He picked up the bottle and their glasses on the way to the parlor settee.

She appeared in the parlor entry. "You know this sort of familiarity is against my better judgment."

"I assure you, I'm a far better judge when it comes to familiarity."

"I was afraid of that." She took a seat beside him, a discreet distance away.

He handed her a freshly filled glass. "How much longer must we maintain this little charade?"

"What charade?"

"The charade that pretends you feel nothing between us."

"I don't know what you're talking about."

"Oh, but you do. The pink in your cheeks and that little pulse in your throat tell no lie."

She put her hands to her cheeks. "It's only the sherry."

"Is it?" Slowly he leaned across the great divide separating them. Her eyes, liquid green, drifted behind lazy lids. He caught her lips in his, ever so lightly. He felt her yield ever so slightly.

"See, I told you it was a charade."

"I'm comfortable with that. I'm not comfortable with . . . this."

Another kiss, more fulsome this time. She

pulled back.

"It's time for me to go to my room before . . ."

"Before what?"

"Before it gets any . . . later."

She was gone. Longstreet smiled after her.

Johnson County

Longstreet drew a halt at midday in the willow breaks along a lazy winding creek.

"I figure Buffalo is another two, maybe three hours' ride. This is probably as good a place as any for you to take a rest."

"All the comforts of home."

"Look for my tack in the livery."

"Who takes the packhorse?"

"I will. Put him up with Yankee."

"See you tonight."

Buffalo

Longstreet stepped down at the livery stable under a bright midafternoon sun. A bent scarecrow of an old-timer with a wild thatch of white hair greeted him.

"What can I do for you, young fella?"

"Need to put up my horse and rent a rig if you've got one available."

"Buckboard do?"

"Will. Lookin' to find a friend who moved here a couple of years ago. You wouldn't happen to know where Maddie O'Rourke lives, would you?"

"White house on West Hart Street. This here's High Street. Take it north. Hart is west just north of town. She'll recognize the buckboard. Rents it herself from time to time. Put your blue and pack animal up in them first two stalls, while I hitch up the buckboard."

"Much obliged." *Hart Street.* Longstreet unsaddled Yankee throwing his tack over a stall post provided for the purpose. He scratched a short note to Cane and tucked it under the saddle blanket.

Thirty minutes later Longstreet wheeled the buckboard west onto Hart. The neatly whitewashed clapboard was the only one of its kind. He drew rein and climbed down. Setting the tie-down, he paused at the gate. *What now, Maddie?*

Boots on the porch sounded louder than his knock.

The door swung open. Emerald eyes misted at the sight of him.

"Beau. You came."

"Of course, I did. Did you doubt it?"

"I had no right to expect it after what I did."

"How are those tried and true rules of yours holding up?"

She rushed into his arms. He held her

138

tight. Two long years of longing spent in fierce embrace.

She pulled back. "Where have my manners gone, come in."

"Oh, I don't know, your manners feel fine to me."

She risked a Mona Lisa smile and led the way to a small parlor. "Have a seat. Can I get you anything?"

"No thank you. I rented the buckboard so we could drive out to the Shaws' place. Briscoe is with me. He's in town trying to get himself hired as a Wyoming Stock Growers Association stock detective. You can fill me in on the situation out here on the ride to the Shaw ranch."

"Let me get my bonnet. I'll only be a minute. And Beau, I feel ever so much better, having you here."

"Glad to hear that."

Buffalo Hotel

The hotel lobby stood deserted in late afternoon. Slanting sunlight filtered through velvet curtains gave the room a red glow. Cane approached the registration desk. A bespectacled clerk with garters banding his shirtsleeves spun the register.

"Room, sir?"

"Maybe. I'm looking for a man may be a

guest here. Jack Black?"

"Mr. Black stays here quite often."

"Is he registered now?"

"As a matter of fact, he is, though I believe he is out on business at the moment."

"Good. I'll have that room then and I'll leave him a note if I might."

"Sign here, please. Room two-oh-four. Top of the stairs on the right."

Cane scratched a note to Black introducing himself as having been sent by Mr. McGant.

"I'll give him the note as soon as he comes in." Glancing at the grandfather clock across the lobby he added, "Should be back anytime now."

"I'll be waiting, soon as I stable my horse."

Shaw Ranch

The buckboard clattered into the yard drawn by a jogging bay. Susan set down her dishcloth and went to the door. Maddie O'Rourke stepped down with the help of a tall handsome stranger.

"Maddie, what brings you out this way?"

"Help, Susan. Susan Shaw, meet Beau Longstreet."

"Pleased to meet you, Mr. Longstreet."

"Please, Beau will do."

"Very well, Beau."

"Is Dan about?" Maddie said.

"He's mending a corral rail behind the barn. Have a seat inside. I'll fetch him."

Out of the bright sunshine the cabin was dim. Seating for four called for the kitchen table. Susan and Dan came in moments later. Beau stood, extending his hand.

"Beau Longstreet, Dan."

"Pleased to meet you. Susan tells me you're a friend of Maddie's."

"Close enough."

"Beau once favored me with a proposal of marriage I wasn't smart enough to accept."

"Her version of it, but that's not why we're here. I have a background in law enforcement. Maddie tells me you are having trouble with the Wyoming Stock Growers Association. She's afraid you might be in danger and asked me to help. Tell me about it."

"We along with many others in Johnson County homestead ranches and farms provided under the Homestead Act on land once left to open range. The big cattle ranchers don't recognize our claims on the land. They are muscling up stock detectives to run us off our land with trumped-up rustling charges, threats, and intimidation. I don't know anyone who hasn't felt the pressure. I gave testimony in one of the rustling

141

cases that led to an acquittal. Likely made me a marked man. The question is, what's to be done about it? All the power and money is on the other side."

"First we need to find out what the other side is up to. I've already taken steps to get to the bottom of that. Second, you need a shadow."

"A shadow? I don't understand."

"I'm your shadow."

"How does that work?"

"Everywhere you go, I'll be close by. You got a place for me to bunk in the barn?"

"There's room to bunk in here."

"Barn's better. It casts your shadow over the whole house. I got a little work to do tonight, but I'll be back tomorrow with my horse. Wait for me before you head out to your day's chores."

"I don't know what to say. We can't pay you to do this."

"No need." He glanced at Maddie. "Call it a favor for a friend."

She blushed a little. Susan stepped in.

"We are ever so grateful to both of you. I know I feel better already."

"We'll do the best we can, Susan. The odds are stacked against us, but maybe we can stay a step ahead of Black and his men. If we can, that may even things up some."

"Beau knows his business, Susan. I too feel better for having him here." Maddie held Beau with her eyes.

CHAPTER FIFTEEN

Denver
1911

Friday after work Penny and I meet at a favored ice-cream parlor for our ritual sundaes in a booth that holds a special sentiment to our love. This day conversation turned to home ownership. Penny savored a spoonful of caramel-topped vanilla to flavor her thinking.

"What are we to do about furniture? Our bed only goes so far."

"I love the destination," I teased.

"Be serious, Robert. Playtime comes later."

I spread hot fudge over the problem. "Whatever we do we shall have to do it economically."

"We must have a table and chairs to eat at."

"Something to sit on in the parlor seems needful too."

"It does. I've browsed the Montgomery Ward catalog. A kitchen set is more affordable than a settee. Settees can be quite costly."

"Did you find a kitchen set you favored?"

"I saw several with possibilities. I'll look some more. We can look at them together tomorrow after your visit with Briscoe."

Several with possibilities, I felt the pressure of wedding choices rear its uncomfortable head once more. I felt the dawn of profound helpless failure anew. *Furnishings,* I should have known. We settled the plan with our usual exchange of spoons, my hot fudge for Penny, her caramel for me. All foretold an exchange of similarly flavored kisses.

Buffalo

Longstreet drove a leisurely pace on the ride back to Maddie's home, giving them the opportunity of small talk.

"Why Buffalo?"

She gazed away wistfully. "Newspaper story. Spoke of the boom in the cattle business around Johnson County. I thought to find opportunity here and I did."

"And the Shaws?"

"Chance meeting at the bank. They'd just been turned down for a loan. I could afford the amount they needed. The investment

145

provides a modest income. Modest is all I need. And you? What have you been up to since . . . ?"

"You left. League work."

"Did you find someone to fill a need in your heart?"

He turned to catch her eye. "You remember the old Beau. The one before you."

"You mean the Beau who made a mockery of my rules?"

"No. That Beau came to be after you. Without you, all that was left is the old Beau."

"I don't know what to say to that."

"Don't say anything. Give it time. Time will tell us everything we need to know. For now, we'd only be guessing."

They drove for a spell in silence.

"If you don't mind, I took the liberty of arranging for Briscoe to meet us at your place tonight. It's best if he and I aren't seen together."

"I don't mind. Gives me a chance to fix you some supper."

"Just like old times."

"Time will tell."

Buffalo Hotel
A knock sounded at the door.

"Who is it?"

"Message for Mr. Cane."

Cane opened the door. Took the note and tipped the desk clerk two bits. He opened the note and read.

Meet me in the bar. I'll be at a corner table with a red-haired man.

Black

Cane had given some thought to his play. He had an angle he figured the association man couldn't resist. The bar crowd was sparse early in the evening. Two men at a corner table were easy enough to spot.

"Jack Black?"

"You Cane?"

"I am."

"Pull up a chair. This here's Red Gates, though most folks call him Rusty." He signaled the bartender for another glass. "So, Buck McGant sent you."

"He said you were hiring stock detectives."

"You an experienced stock detective?"

"No, just handy."

The bartender set down a glass for Cane.

Black scowled, reaching for the bottle. "Just handy. Handy with what?"

"Guns, knives, the usual."

Black poured. "What makes you think that

qualifies for stock detective work?"

"I read the papers. Doesn't take much readin' between the lines to figure what you're up to. If you don't need the usual, there's always the unusual."

"Oh? What unusual?"

Cane smiled. "Dynamite."

"Dynamite, hmm, what ya think, Rusty?"

"Might could come in handy."

"Might could. Some of them stumps is rooted pretty deep. Alright, Cane, you good enough for Buck McGant, you're good enough for me. Sixty a month."

"What have stumps got to do with stock detective work?"

"Squatters root deep as a stump. You can start tomorrow. Meet us at the livery at sunup."

Longstreet folded his napkin.

"Best meal I've had in quite a spell."

"Nothing fancy."

"Doesn't need to be in good company."

Maddie blushed a little beneath the light touch of freckle sprinkling her nose.

Longstreet rose. "Let me give you a hand with these dishes."

"No need. Have a seat in the parlor."

"After the dishes are done, we can both have a seat. Sort of like old times."

"Never did have much control when it came to you, did I?"

"Never noticed."

"That's what I mean."

Dishes done, they took to the parlor. Maddie sat, silent hands folded in her lap. Beau too at something of a loss for words. The unsaid hung like a velvet drape between them. Mercifully the sound of a horse drew rein outside. Longstreet drew back a lace window curtain.

"Briscoe's here." He opened the door. "You found it alright?"

"Livery rig parked out front is clue enough even for me." He stepped inside. "Maddie, good to see you again."

"You too, Briscoe. Thank you for coming with Beau. I feel so much better knowing you are with him."

"So, you in the stock detective business?"

"I am. Met Black and a fella they call Rusty Gates, couple hours ago."

"Rusty Gates?"

"Red hair."

"Any problem getting them to take you on?"

"Didn't pretend to any stock detective experience. Tempted them with one of my lesser known talents."

"Explosives."

"We been workin' together too long, Long-street."

"So, what are we up against?"

Cane glanced at Maddie.

"No need to sugarcoat it on my account. I knew there was a need to call for help."

"They're fixin' to play rough. We're ridin' somewhere at sunup."

"Any idea where?"

"Not exactly, though Black did make a comment to Gates I heard as we were breakin' up about Shaw knowin' too much."

"Maddie took me out to the Shaw place this afternoon. Nice folks. By morning you can count on me bein' Dan's shadow. If they're headed to the Shaw place you're on the inside and I'm on the outside. Leave the first option up to me, so you stay undercover as long as possible. No tellin' how many acts there is to this play."

"We play it by ear then. It would help if we had some way to stay in contact as the need arises. The sheriff would work for you, but I don't know I should be frequenting his office."

"True. Any other ideas?"

"How about me?" Maddie said. "Black and Gates don't know who I am, let alone my relationship to the Shaws."

"I don't like it." Beau said. "Puts you in

the middle of this. I won't have you put at risk again. Look where it got us the last time."

"I'm already at risk."

"How so?"

"By putting you at risk."

"She's got a point, Beau."

"I still don't like it."

"I insist."

"You two work out your side of things. If I need to get word to you, Beau, Maddie will have it. Best I get on back to town before I'm missed." Briscoe tipped his hat. "Maddie."

Longstreet met his eyes. "You be careful, hear?"

"You too."

Longstreet let him out. "I best get the livery rig back to town. I'll need Yankee in the morning."

"Where will you stay?"

"I've slept in a hayloft before."

"Beau." She wrung her hands, lifted eyes misty in soft lamplight. "Thank you for coming. I'm so glad you are here. I had no right . . ."

He reached her in one stride. She melted into his arms. Tears streaming down her cheeks. He held her.

"It's gonna be alright. You'll see."

She straightened up. "Take that rig into town. Ride Yankee back here. That settee isn't much, but it's better than a hayloft. I'll leave the door unlatched."

"You sure you are comfortable with that?"

"I still have my rules. You haven't abridged them all, yet."

"I'll likely be gone before you are up."

"Just be careful then." She tipped up on her toes to brush a soft kiss against his cheek.

He held her eyes. Moments passed unspoken. He squeezed her shoulders, stepping into the night air.

Maddie slipped into her night dress, closed the bedroom door, and huffed out the bedside lamp. She crawled beneath the covers; resting her head on her pillow she gazed into the darkened ceiling. *The old Beau Longstreet.*

"Maddie O'Rourke, may I present Sarah Mc-Bride."

Maddie crossed the dining room, wiping her hands on her apron. Her lips smiled. Her eyes were not amused. Now what have we got up to here?

"Sarah's just arrived in Denver. She's in need of a room. Briscoe suggested you might have one." The explanation came out too fast. It sounded a bit forced. It was.

"Briscoe, is it? Nice to meet you, Miss McBride. It is 'Miss,' isn't it?"

"Why, yes. Nice to meet you, too, Mrs. O'Rourke."

"Did you come in on the Santa Fe stage with Beau here?"

"I did. And fortunate I was to have him and Mr. Cane to save us from those horrible stage robbers."

"He does know his way around trouble. What happened?"

The question had an Irish edge. "We think El Anillo tried to liberate our prisoner."

"I see. How fortunate for Miss McBride to have had you there in her time of need."

Sarah puzzled at the tone. "Have you a room then, Mrs. O'Rourke?"

"I'm afraid not, my dear."

Longstreet clenched hold of the drop in his jaw.

"Pity, you have such a lovely home here. Would you know of any other respectable residences I might try?"

"I'm sorry, my dear, I don't. Might you, Beau?"

"At the moment, I can only suggest the Palace."

"Well, thank you both for your kindness. I can find my way back to the station."

"Good day, Miss McBride."

153

Longstreet watched her go. "You do have a vacant room."

"Of course."

"Then why not . . . ?"

"I'll not have that go on under my very nose."

"That? What 'that'?"

"You know perfectly well, what that."

"Oh, that that."

"Yes, that that."

"There ain't no that to go on."

"Not in this house."

"Of that we can be sure," Beau said.

"We can," Maddie said.

"You know this conversation makes absolutely no sense . . . unless —"

"Unless what?"

"Unless . . . you know."

"I don't know."

"I think you do."

"I've no idea what you are talking about, Beau Longstreet."

"Unless you're jealous."

"Jealous? Nothing could be further from the truth."

"Oh? I don't know."

"Well, I do."

"I'm pleased to hear that. You know you're lovely with that flour smear on your cheek."

"Rrrgh!" She wiped her cheek with the back of a fist.

"Other cheek."
She turned on her heel.
"Missed me, too."
She stomped back to the kitchen.

She smiled at the memory. He'd caught her up in the deceit of her feelings. Feelings she'd struggled desperately to deny. In the end they'd become undeniable. The front door opened. She warmed to the thought of Beau in her house. He would ride into danger before dawn. Danger she brought him to. Now who's making a mockery of the rules? She'd put him at risk. In doing so, she put herself at risk of the very loss that frightened her away from happiness once. Now he was here. It could be her second chance. Did she have the courage? Did Beau still have feelings? As he said, *time will tell.*

CHAPTER SIXTEEN

Shaw Ranch

Longstreet rode in gray light before dawn. He stabled Yankee in the barn and took up his watch. *Maddie.* He'd taken her offer of the settee. It felt good to know she was nearby. So good he hadn't slept worth a damn. The question gnawed at him. *Where to from here?* Seeing her opened a wound he thought healed. He never considered the possibility from the moment he opened her letter. Never considered the possibility. And then it was done and the only thing that mattered is that he would see her again.

Dan Shaw started his day with the sun to find Longstreet on watch in the barn without knowing he'd called him back from afar.

"You're up before the birds."

"Got here before sunrise. What do you have planned for today?"

"Holding pen in my southwest section needs some repair."

156

"Alright, here's how this works. You go about your business. I keep watch out of sight. If I see trouble coming, I fire a warning shot. You head for home while I cover your back trail."

"What kind of trouble you figure we might have?"

"The kind that silences someone who knows too much."

Black drew a halt west of Clear Creek and the Shaw Ranch.

"Split up we got a better chance of finding him. Rusty, you ride south and east. Cane and me will ride north. If'n you find him, you know what to do."

Black led north. Gates swung south.

Cane tucked Smoke just off Black's stirrup. "What makes this Shaw guy a target?"

"He's a squatter like the rest. Uppity though. He bucked us on rustlin' charges we brought against one of 'em. Testified in court. Made us look like we mixed the stolen cattle in with the herd where we found them."

"Did you?"

"What do you think?"

"Don't matter what I think. What did the jury think?"

"Jury," Black spit. "Just a bunch of sodbusters an' rustlers theirselves. We aim to put the fear of God in all of 'em. Startin' with too smart for his own good Dan Shaw."

Longstreet set himself up in a stand of white oak atop a knoll overlooking the holding pen Dan set to work on. The hilltop view afforded him a good look south and west, the two most likely approaches coming out of Buffalo. Longstreet used a glass to extend his search for sign. The morning waned hot and dry. Toward noon a wisp of dust appeared in the west, headed southeasterly toward them. The dust trail in the glass resolved into a horse and rider. Soon enough a rider with red hair. Had to be the one Cane called Rusty Gates.

Longstreet fired the agreed warning shot. The rider pulled up, likely trying to figure where the shot came from. Dan mounted up and lit out for home as planned. A dust plume like the one that gave up Gates, gave Gates Dan. The stock detective spurred up a gallop after him. Longstreet swung into the saddle. Unable to get between Dan and the stockman, Longstreet took up pursuit with considerable ground to make up. Thankfully Dan had a good start on his pursuer.

Bent on catching Dan, Gates didn't hear

or see his own pursuer. As soon as he had himself in something close to pistol range Gates drew and fired. A long-range pistol shot from the back of a galloping horse had little chance of hitting its mark. It didn't.

Longstreet closed. He let out a loop in his riata. Gates heard hoofbeats closing. He turned in the saddle, too late to bring his gun into play as Longstreet's long lazy loop pinned his arms to his sides. Yankee's slide-stop jerked Gates from the saddle. The hard fall knocked the wind out of him and sent his gun spinning into the sagebrush.

Longstreet swung down, letting Yankee hold his man. He had cuffs on Gates before the man found his breath.

"Who the hell are you and what do you think you're doin'?"

"I'm your arresting officer and you're under arrest for the attempted murder of Dan Shaw."

"I don't know what you're talkin' about."

"We're talking about the shot you fired at Dan while illegally trespassing on his property. On your feet. We're going to see the sheriff."

Longstreet collected the discharged pistol, putting the evidence in his saddlebag. He helped Gates up on his horse as Dan rode up.

"You got him."

"Did, though he got closer than I planned."

"What now?"

"Now he belongs to the sheriff. You best come along with me. It's likely his partner is out here somewhere, and I can't be in two places at once. You keep an eye on him while I keep an eye on our back trail."

Sheriff's Office
Buffalo

Sheriff Ben Whitaker sat at his desk. A solidly built man with watery blue eyes and drooping gray mustaches. He stood, revealing a sight paunch hung over his gun belt as Dan Shaw and a big stranger trooped through the door with an ill-humored Red Gates in handcuffs.

"What's this all about, Dan?"

"I'll let Mr. Longstreet explain. Beau Longstreet, meet Sheriff Ben Whitaker."

"Sheriff, I'm an officer of the Great Western Detective League. Are you familiar with our organization?"

"Heard of it. Good things too."

"I'm here to look after the Shaws out of a concern their lives might be in danger. This afternoon, I observed Gates here attempt to bushwhack Dan. Here is the pistol he used.

I was able to subdue him before he got off more than one shot. Dan and I will fill out a complaint on him. You need to lock him up."

"Fair enough. This way, Gates."

"You got no call to do this, Sheriff. That big jasper jumped me for no reason. My gun discharged when he roped me off my horse."

"Save it for the judge and jury."

"Kangaroo court more like it in this town."

A cell door clanged to a jangle of keys.

Buffalo Hotel

Cane swung through the batwings to the bar. Black sat at a corner table alone.

"Where's Gates?"

"Good question. He hasn't come back." Black poured Cane a drink and refilled his own glass.

"You think Shaw might have got him?"

"That squatter? Rusty may not be the best man around, but he's way too good for that."

"What do you figure to do?"

"If he ain't back by morning, we ride out to the Shaw place and have a look for ourselves. You want to have some supper?"

"Pass if you don't mind. Met a lady. Well you know."

"Knock yourself out. Just be ready to ride at sunup."

Cane left the bar headed for the livery stable.

Hart Street

Maddie sat alone in her lamplit parlor, a favored book of poetry open in her lap. She couldn't concentrate. Something must have happened. Enough to cause Briscoe to leave her with a warning message for Beau. What happened? Was Beau alright? Would he come tonight? Hope mingled with fear. Fear she understood. *Hope.* She wanted to see him again. She remembered the Beau who'd made her feel *uncomfortable.* She remembered the feel of discomfort with *fondness.* Why was he so damnably disturbing? Why did she reach out to him at the first sign of trouble? *Why? Foolish question, girl. You know perfectly well why. It's only the admission that's a problem.*

Tack jangled a horse to a halt outside. A little pulse jumped in her throat. She reached the door before he knocked and let him in quickly.

"What happened? Is everyone alright? I'm so relieved you're here."

"Easy now. Everyone is fine. Gates tried to bushwhack Dan. We got him. He's cool-

162

ing his heels in jail charged with attempted murder."

"That's good news."

"So far. I'll wager you have a message from Briscoe."

"I do. Gates never returned from the Shaws' place. That makes sense now. If he doesn't come back by morning, which he won't, Black and Briscoe are planning to ride out to the ranch to find out what happened."

"Good. When Black finds out Gates is in jail, it will likely smoke out more of what the big boys have in mind."

"You think there is more to this than Black and Gates?"

"I'm sure of it."

"Then I shall have to maintain my watch of worry."

"Well, I should be getting back to the Shaws."

"Couldn't you . . . stay for just a bit?"

He tilted his chin at an amused angle. "On one condition."

"Oh, oh."

"I'll be right back."

She watched his broad-shouldered dark shadow walk to the gate to rummage in his saddlebag before returning. He stepped inside and closed the door, holding a bottle of amber whiskey to lamplight.

"You must join me."

"My rules."

"Made to be broken, for the good Irish you prefer."

"Do you ever change?"

"Do you want me to? I offered that once to no good effect."

"I don't believe I do."

"Want a drink?"

"No. You to change. Now give me the bottle. Have a seat. I'll fetch some glasses."

Beau made the ride back to the Shaw Ranch at an easy pace, savoring a bright moonlit night and the taste of Maddie's kiss fresh on his lips. They had some of their best moments with him taking his leave . . .

She came to the door of his room to find him feverishly packing at midmorning.

"In again, out again, gone again, Finnegan."

"What?"

"Old Irish saying for a sailor gone to sea. Where to this time?"

"Santa Fe."

"Perhaps I should just rent you a closet. It would save you some money, and I could rent out this room to someone who might actually use it."

He paused with a smile. "You do miss me."

She clenched her fists on her hips. "Why are you so obsessed with me missing you?"

"I'm not. I'm obsessed with you."

"When you're not otherwise obsessed."

He threw up his hands and turned to his packing. "Maybe she's right after all."

"Who's right?"

"Samantha."

"Her again. Will she be going to Santa Fe?"

"Can't say. Doesn't matter. There's nothing between us."

"You say. What's she so right about this time?"

"She doesn't know which one of us is the greater fool. You for not knowing what you're missing, or me for knowing and not . . ." It took only one long stride to sweep her up in his arms. You couldn't exactly call her resistance a struggle. More like an annoyed wriggle until the kiss melted.

She gasped, holding him as tightly as he held her. "You are a thoroughly vexing man, Beau Longstreet."

"Pleasantly so, given half the chance."

"Perhaps . . . I am the fool."

"Beautifully so." He kissed her again.

"Now, about that closet: have you one available in your room?"

"I give in for a penny, and you ask for the whole of a pound."

"I'm a patient man, Maddie O'Rourke. Patient and persistent."

"I can see that." She tipped up on her toes, risked a small smile, and kissed him.

"Miss me."

"I shall consider it."

He closed his case and dashed down the stairs. Satisfied he'd left her thoroughly . . . vexed.

Shaw Ranch

Dan found Longstreet in the barn at first light.

"Wouldn't you be more comfortable bunking in the house?"

"Maybe, but I'm more useful out here. Anybody comes calling, I got your back. Speaking of visitors, Briscoe left a message for me with Maddie last night. Black and Cane are coming to call to find out what happened to Gates. There are two ways to play this. You get a vote."

"I'm listening."

"Pretty clear they want you out of the way. Can't rule out Black may make that play today. I'll have your back. On one play, I take him out, either kill him or arrest him. That eliminates the immediate threat. It doesn't end your troubles with the cattle growers."

166

"And the other play?"

"We run 'em off. Briscoe still has his cover, so we'll know their next move. Ending your troubles and those of your neighbors depends on rooting out the people behind all this. Black and Gates are nothing more than foot soldiers. We need the generals. You're the one with the target on your back. How do you want to play it?"

"Keep Susan safe no matter what happens."

"Count on it."

Nigh on noon Black and Cane rode into the yard. Dan stepped out of the cabin.

"What you want, Black?"

"Lookin' for Rusty Gates. He was last seen headed your way."

"With murder on his mind."

"You say. Either way looks like he didn't have much luck with that. Where is he?"

"He ain't here. You really want to find him, check with Sheriff Whitaker."

"What's Whitaker got to do with this?"

"He's holding him on attempted murder charges, as if you didn't know."

"And you'd be just the witness to convict him."

"Figured that out all by yourself, did you?"

167

Black drew his gun. "Dead men don't talk."

"Black! I got two barrels of double-ought buck. One for each of you. Drop your gun, now!"

Black turned his head to the barn.

"Drop it!"

He did. "Who the hell are you?"

"Your arresting officer, if you don't get your sorry asses off this man's land."

Black wheeled his horse. "This ain't over."

Cane tipped his hat and swung in at Black's back.

CHAPTER SEVENTEEN

O'Rourke House
1911

Angela answered my knock, wiping flour-caked hands on her apron. The smell of baking bread filled the house with the feeling of home.

"Robert, come in."

"Sure, smells good in here."

"Won't be long before you have fresh baked bread in your new home."

"That will be nice, once we've figured out the furnishing part. Furniture is expensive."

"I saw notice of Ethel David's estate sale in the *Tribune.* Perhaps you can find a bargain or two from furnishings already in the house."

"That is a good idea. We've been shopping the Montgomery Ward catalog. There are so many choices. It reminds me of all the decisions that went into our wedding, decisions I confess I am not very good at."

"Not to worry. You got through the wedding decisions by being supportive of Penny's preferences. You'll do so again while furnishing your new home."

A stair creaked underfoot. "Good afternoon, Robert. Shall we begin before Angela talks your ear off?"

"Before I talk his ear off. It's you who'll drone the afternoon away."

"Ah, but there is purpose in my droning, as you put it, and you my dear shall hang on my every word."

"My dear, indeed."

I handed Briscoe his weekly bottle as we repaired to the parlor.

Cattlemen's Club
Cheyenne

"Black needs help," Buck McGant said.

"What now?" Davis Chesterfield nodded a cloud of fragrant cigar smoke.

"Got a telegram this afternoon. Gates is in jail, charged with the attempted murder of Dan Shaw."

"Attempted murder."

"Attempted is right. Shaw signed the complaint along with some stranger who's watchin' Shaw's back."

"What's to be done about it?"

"We need professional help. Gates can't

170

go to trial. As long as Shaw is around to testify, there's a trail that leads to us."

"You got someone in mind?"

"I do."

"Who?"

"Tom Dorn."

"Never heard of him."

"That's why he's a professional."

"What makes him so good?"

"Crack shot, you'd expect. They say he can track a fart in a blizzard. Always gets his man. Never been caught or charged with anything."

"How many kills?"

"Only he knows."

Cattlemen's Club
Two weeks later

McGant arranged a private room on the second floor. He sent Black to the depot to meet Dorn with instructions to bring him to the club using the back stairs. McGant and Chesterfield waited in a nicely appointed card room with full bar, reserved for high-stakes private games. Both sipped whiskies in cut crystal glasses. A soft knock sounded at the door.

"Come." McGant summoned.

Black led the way accompanied by a tall, lean figure of a man in gray mourning attire. Weathered features, angular and lined, said little to distinguish him apart from cold gray eyes that missed little. McGant indicated a chair.

"Tom Dorn, meet Buck McGant and Davis Chesterfield. Mr. McGant is president of the Wyoming Stock Growers Association. Mr. Chesterfield is treasurer."

Dorn nodded.

"Thank you for coming," McGant began.

"No thanks to it. You know my price."

"Worth our problem. Jack here can fill you in on the situation we face in Johnson County. You can take your direction up there from him. As we understand your terms, your fees are five hundred dollars on contract, five hundred dollars on completion, with one hundred dollars per day for any days over ten. Is that correct?"

"It is."

"Davis."

Chesterfield reached in his coat pocket, drew out a thick envelope, and passed it to Dorn. Dorn opened the envelope flap, fanned the notes, and slipped the envelope in his coat pocket.

"Everything in order?" McGant asked.

Dorn nodded.

"Then good hunting."

Dorn rose and followed Black to the door.

"One more thing, Mr. Dorn."

He paused.

"This meeting never happened."

Another nod and he was gone.

Davis refilled their glasses. "Not a very talkative sort, is he?"

"Best kind of killer."

Hart Street
Buffalo

Maddie sat on the porch swing under a star-splashed black velvet sky. A pleasant evening breeze brushed away the heat of the day. Wispy tendrils of auburn hair fluttered on the breeze. Down the street, hooves clip-clopped a brisk beat. Horse and rider cloaked in shadow resolved out of the night. A flicker of excitement she tried to deny leapt involuntarily up the back of her throat.

Beau drew up and stepped down, looping Yankee's rein over the fence. Starlight shone on her pale-yellow dress, her face and features veiled in shadow.

"Evenin'."

"Evenin' yourself, cowboy." She slid over to one side of the seat. "Care for a swing?"

"Don't mind if I do."

"Hoped you'd come by."

"You did?"

"Briscoe came by the other day."

"Oh, for a minute there I thought you hoped I'd come by."

"Well maybe that too."

"We'll get back to that thought directly. What's was on Briscoe's mind?"

"He thinks something is up. He doesn't know what yet, but after you ran Black off the Shaw place, Black had sudden business in Cheyenne. Briscoe says he'll know more when Black gets back."

"He say when that might be?"

"He didn't."

"Uh-oh."

"Uh-oh, what?"

"Uh-oh, I'll need to come by more regular then."

"Uh-oh."

"That scary?"

"That depends."

"Depends on what?"

"I don't know. I'll have to think it over."

"I think better with a little of that Irish you favor."

"I'm sure you do. Now that I think about it. Stay put. I'll be back in two shakes."

Two of the prettiest shakes a man could imagine.

Two shakes later she handed him a glass and took her seat. He offered her his rim. She touched hers to it.

"Here's to uh-oh."

"I said I had to think it over."

"Then here's to risking an uh-oh."

"Now that I can drink to." Swallows followed.

"How about we start with dinner tomorrow night?"

"Best offer I've had since the last time you made supper for me."

"Careful or you'll turn a girl's head."

"I'm trying."

"You can certainly say that again."

"That unpleasant, is it?"

"It's that old comfort thing."

"Ah, as I recall, I get comfortable and that makes you uncomfortable."

"Something like that."

"As I recall, we worked our way through that once."

"You're very reminiscent tonight."

"Pleasant memories."

"Pleasant memories make you comfortable?"

"They do. Pleasant present makes me comfortable too."

"I was afraid of that."

"Worse than uncomfortable?"

"Supper tomorrow night?"

"Supper."

CHAPTER EIGHTEEN

Buffalo Hotel

Cane entered the hotel bar. Black sat at his favored corner table along with a tall stranger. Black waved Cane over, signaling the bartender for another glass. He pulled up a chair.

"Briscoe Cane, meet Tom Dorn."

The men exchanged glances.

"Tom's here to give us a hand with our particular problem. Comes highly recommended."

"Good to hear." *Tom Dorn.*

"Tom, I think it might be best if Briscoe went along with you tomorrow. Might bring your hunt to a quick conclusion."

"I work alone. No offense, Cane."

"None taken."

"You sure, Tom?"

"I work alone." He tossed off his drink. "You'll hear from me when I finish." He

176

pushed his chair away from the table and left.

Black watched him go.

"Friendly sort," Cane said.

"Still might be best if you tagged along, welcome or not. Shaw's got somebody lookin' after him. You might put an edge on the odds."

"I'll pick up his trail when he leaves town in the morning. I'll keep an eye on things."

"Good."

Tom Dorn. Need to get to Maddie's.

Hart Street

Maddie waited at the window. She opened the door as Longstreet stepped down. She held the door anxiously as he strode up the walk.

"I'm so glad you're here."

"Like the sound of that."

"Not like that. Briscoe was here." She closed the door, leading the way to the parlor settee. She sat, stiffened, hands clasped in her lap.

"What did he have to say?"

"Black is back. He brought a man named Tom Dorn with him."

"Dorn, heard of him."

"Briscoe says he is an assassin for hire."

"That's what I heard of him. Did Briscoe

say how we should play this?"

"He said, Dorn works alone. Briscoe plans to follow him. Black thinks Briscoe will give Dorn an edge if you were to see him coming. If Dorn gets close, Briscoe will take care of the threat. You'll have to take credit with the sheriff to keep his cover from being blown."

"Makes sense."

"Scares the life out of me. A professional killer. What won't these people do?"

"Bad people do bad things. Been that way since Cain felled Abel. That's why Briscoe and I do what we do."

"I understand the need, but does it have to be . . . does it have to be someone?" She twisted her hands, chin lifted to him, moist in her gaze. "Does it have to be someone I love? There, I said it."

He took her in his arms and held her. She trembled against him. Time stood still.

"I'm being silly, aren't I."

He lifted her chin. "I love you too. There I said it. Nothing silly about it."

She smiled, misty-eyed. Two years of thirst dissolved in a kiss. Breathless, "Here we are, right back where we started, aren't we?"

His gaze traveled to some middle distance. "I'm not so sure. Feels like we're back where we belong. Never felt like this before in all my life, Maddie O'Rourke. I'm changed. Like it or not. Will you risk loving me?"

"I've already taken that risk. Yes. Only please be careful. I lost you once for fear of losing you. Not a day went by I didn't regret the loss. I'll not lose you again."

"Nor I you."

The moment went lost in a surge of gauzy magic.

"Oh dear," Maddie breathed. "My rules. They're all but in tatters again."

"I've been accused of having that effect."

"Please."

Lingering.

"Tomorrow."

"Tomorrow?"

"Be careful."

"Just for you."

Shaw Ranch

In the quiet of first light the barn smelled of sweet hay and horse scents. Dan opened the barn door silhouetted in sunlight. Longstreet worked the latigo, saddling Yankee.

"Where we headed today?"

Longstreet regarded him under the brim of his hat. "You aren't going anywhere except back in the house to lay low. Briscoe tells me Black is back along with Tom Dorn."

"Who's he?"

"Professional assassin. About now he's mounting up to go hunting."

"Hunting who?"

"You."

"What are we going to do?"

"We aren't doing anything. I'm riding out to impersonate you."

"You're fixin' to make yourself a target for a professional assassin."

"Yup."

"If you don't mind my sayin', you getting yourself killed is no help on my account."

"I don't intend to get myself killed."

"How can you be so sure?"

"Briscoe is backing my play."

"Still sounds mighty risky."

"Life is risky in this line of work." *Risky.* The word sounded involuntary alarm. "One more thing before you go back in the house. Not a word about this to Maddie. Understood?"

"Understood."

"Susan too."

"Susan too."

Longstreet kept his glass on the road up from town. An hour past sunup a lone rider

180

showed in the distance. He let him come close enough he couldn't be missed wheeling out from behind a low hillock and setting a trail north. *Sure hope Briscoe didn't oversleep.*

North led to hill country, dotted in stands of white oak and river willow. The idea was to keep as much terrain and cover as possible between himself and Dorn. Make the man work for his shot, assuming he took the bait. He rode into the first copse of white oak he could find to check his back trail. A whisp of dust told him he had a tail.

Morning wore on. Dorn seemed in no hurry. Longstreet began searching for a setting to tempt him. A stream with a rocky outcropping on the near bank looked promising. A stop to rest and water his horse beside a good place of cover should he need it. He stepped down on the creek bank to let Yankee drink and wait. He checked his watch, guessing Dorn ten minutes behind him.

He got a sense of it when the birds went quiet. He picked up a pebble on the creek bank and stepped around the rock outcropping, making himself a smaller target. He checked his watch again. Five minutes or so to get in position. Need to allow all that and a little bit more for Briscoe to do the same before letting the ball drop. He waited to the gentle gurgle of the creek, marking the passage of time on the face of his watch.

Fifty yards downstream Dorn crouched in the rocks along the creek bank beside a willow break. He thought he'd have a better shot than he did. The big blue roan stood between him and Shaw. Whatever the hell the man was doing in those rocks didn't help either. He'd get his shot when the rancher remounted his horse. For now, all he could do was wait.

Cane followed at a distance. He dared not get too close for fear of being discovered. When Dorn made no move toward the ranch house, he guessed Beau had set him on a trail of some kind. He eased Smoke into a faster pace. If Dorn got a whiff of a shot, he'd need to move fast. He eased his Henry out of its saddle boot and levered a round into the chamber.

Rounding a low hill, he pulled up. Dorn's horse stood tethered to a river willow with no sign of the killer. He must have gone ahead on foot. Using the tree line along the creek bed for cover Cane rode in as close as he dared. He ground-tied Smoke in the trees and set off on foot. Cane reached the creek bank at the edge of the willow break. Up the rock-strewn bank in the distance he could make out Yankee. No sign of Beau. His eyes worked their way back down the bank to . . . there. What might have been just another gray rock was a hat. A hat with the muzzle of a big bore Sharps rifle.

Cane watched and waited. Time passed. He weighed the possibility of moving in to get the drop on the killer. He judged the noise risk on rocky terrain too great for being caught out. Beau had the play to give him a shot.

Longstreet appeared from behind some rocks near Yankee. Dorn took aim. Cane's Henry cracked. Beau ducked. The Sharps barked. The big fifty gouged a chunk out of rock where his head should have been; the heavy slug whined away, showering Longstreet in stone chips.

"That you, Briscoe?"

"You alright?"

"Little dusty. How's our friend?"

"Checkin' now." Cane moved up the creek bed, rifle leveled at the spot where he'd seen the hat. The Sharps barrel lay at an odd angle. The hat was gone. The exit wound shattered Dorn's forehead, splattering brain on the rocks that had hidden him. "He's out. I'll fetch Smoke and his horse. See if you can drag the body out the other side of the willow break."

Thirty minutes later they had Dorn's body slung over his saddle.

"Give me a start back to town. I'll tell Black you got him before he could kill Shaw. Take the body in to the sheriff. There's enough wanted dodgers out on this jasper to get you a no-questions-asked gold medal."

CHAPTER NINETEEN

Buffalo Hotel

Cane met Black in a deserted hotel saloon.

"Did Dorn get him?"

"Dorn's dead."

"Dead? What happened?"

"I followed him like you said. He cut Shaw's trail and followed him. Shaw stopped to water his horse. Dorn moved in for a shot. Best I could tell somebody cut Dorn's trail ahead of me. I heard two shots. Dorn's Sharps had to be the second by the sound of it. I took cover to see what happened. Next thing I saw was Shaw and a big stranger load Dorn's body on his horse. I lit out for town before they spotted me."

"Son of a bitch. Shaw's got more lives than a cat. McGant's gonna be pissed."

"What do we do next?"

"Wire McGant. See how he wants to play it from here. I'll let you know when I know."

Black scraped back his chair and headed

out to the Western Union office. On the boardwalk he spotted a big stranger on a blue roan ride in leading a horse with a body draped over the saddle. *So that's who we're up against.*

Sheriff's Office

Longstreet found Sheriff Ben Whitaker at his desk having just returned from lunch.

"Beau, what brings you by this time?"

"Got Tom Dorn out there draped over his saddle."

"Dorn, sounds familiar."

"Should. There's more dead or alive dodgers on him than fleas on a good coon dog."

"What'd he do this time?"

"Attempted murder, Dan Shaw."

"Seems like Dan's a marked man."

"He is. He testifies against Gates in there it likely implicates some cattle growers association bigwigs. Dorn doesn't come cheap. Somebody's damn sure determined Dan doesn't testify."

"You're right about the big boys playin' rough when they're of a mind to."

"Maybe we should sweat him some."

"Good idea. Let me get Dorn over to the undertaker and we can take a turn at it."

"I'm gonna get a bite to eat. I'll be back soon as I do."

The cell block door groaned open. Gates stood at his cell window gazing through the bars.

"You got a visitor, Gates."

He looked over his shoulder, sour recognition dawning. "What do you want?"

"How about you scratch my back and I scratch yours."

"My back don't itch."

"It should. You're lookin' at life to a hemp necktie."

"You got to get me to trial first and then get a conviction to go with it."

"We got witnesses seen you do it."

"For now."

"If you're referring to Dan Shaw not making it to court, your pals aren't havin' much luck with that. Somebody hired Tom Dorn to kill him. Ever heard of Dorn?"

"No."

"Professional assassin. About as good as they come. Or should I say came. Sheriff Whitaker just took him to the undertaker, not Dan Shaw."

"So?"

"You know who's behind all this. How big a fall do you plan to take for Black and whoever pulls his strings? Now if you were to tell us who those big boys are, things might be made to go easier on you."

The outer office door opened to Jack Black.
  "Sheriff."
  "Black. What's on your mind?"
  "Need to speak with Rusty."
  "He's busy."
  "He's in jail."
  "He's got a visitor."
  "What sort of visitor?"
  "Great Western Detective League officer."
  "What's he want with Rusty?"
  "Talk."
  "Talk?"
  "Just talk. You can catch Gates later this afternoon."
  Black turned on his heel. Back out on the boardwalk misgiving gnawed at the back of his mind. *What's Rusty got needs talkin' to some detective? Nothin' good I can think of. He wouldn't talk. Would he?*

Hart Street
Early evening sun drifted toward pink and orange topped mountains purpled in shadow. Longstreet wheeled Yankee up to Maddie's gate and stepped down, looping a rein over the fence. He loosened the cinch

and reached for the gate as Maddie rushed down the walkway into his arms.

"I was so worried."

"No need." He breathed in her hair. "Dorn's on his way to pushin' up daisies."

She tipped up her toes and kissed him. "Good."

"Hmm, I'd say good start."

She wrinkled her nose with a smile. "Stay for supper?"

"You need to ask? Glad you did."

"Me too." She took his arm up the walk to the house. Inside they were greeted by a warm golden glow. "Have a seat. I'll get you a little of that Irish to relax while I fix us something to eat."

"You're going to spoil me."

"I'm going to try," she said, pouring his drink.

"A fella could get used to this."

"I hope so."

"One bit of business before we have a pleasant evening. Next time Briscoe comes by, tell him we can trust Sheriff Whitaker should the need arise."

"That's good to know. I thought you might be able to."

"What's for supper?"

"I stopped by the butcher shop today. I think they're called steaks."

189

"Now I know I'm bein' spoiled."

The sizzle of meat smoking fragrantly on a cast-iron skillet drew Longstreet to the kitchen table with his drink.

"You'd be more comfortable in the parlor."

"I'm more comfortable near you."

"Uh-oh."

"Uncomfortable?"

"Not as much."

"Good."

"Was Dan in any danger today?"

"Briscoe and I had the situation covered."

"I'm glad he's with you. I worry less."

"We're off duty now."

"We are?"

"We are. Time to enjoy the wonderful supper you're cookin' and appreciate being together."

"If you say so. Can't believe I said that."

"Darn near out of character."

"Two can play the change game."

"Like the sound of that, though I might miss your feisty side."

"Who said I was giving that up? Don't get ahead of yourself, Beau Longstreet. You haven't won yet."

"Ahead of myself? Perish the thought."

15 Aspen Lane
Denver
1911

We went to the estate sale as Angela suggested. Mrs. David turned it over to a man who did auctions and such. With our budget tight as it was, owing to purchase of the house itself, we agreed to confine our interest to a kitchen set and a settee. We knew from our catalog shopping the settee would be the more expensive of the pieces while the kitchen set filled the more utilitarian need.

"The settee is lovely, despite a bit of wear. The dark blue upholstery is very rich looking, don't you think?"

Somehow, I'd never managed to think of a settee as rich, no matter the color. "It is. Is it a color you might carry on to other furnishing selections?"

"Very clever, Robert. You have a knack for this."

One of those inspired guesses I stumbled on a time or two in planning our wedding. "How much is it?"

Penny lifted a small yellow tag. "Sixty dollars."

"Oh dear."

"Half the price of catalog new."

"Yes, but we'd have precious little left for

a kitchen set."

"Let's have a look at that."

We did. I could tell the one in Mrs. David's kitchen did not inspire my Penny's taste.

"It's . . . functional."

"How much is it?"

Again, the yellow tag.

"Fifteen dollars."

"Price seems fair."

"I don't suppose we could do both."

"I'm afraid not at the moment."

"The sale of course will end before we have time to afford both."

"The settee then is the greater value."

"It's four times the price of the kitchen set."

"But we save sixty dollars off the catalog price and we don't even have to move it."

"What will we do about a kitchen set?"

"I don't love this one. We shall simply figure something out." She turned to the salesman. "We'll take the settee."

Most expensive sixty dollars I ever saved.

CHAPTER TWENTY

Cattlemen's Club
Cheyenne

McGant and Chesterfield sat in oversized wing chairs in the private gaming room, cigars and whiskey in hand.

Chesterfield swirled amber liquid in cut glass, savoring the aroma. "Some professional."

"Best money could buy."

"Five-hundred-dollar pauper's grave is damned expensive."

"How can one little shit squatter be so much trouble?" McGant said through a cloud of fragrant cigar smoke.

"He's got help. Competent help. The question is who and why."

"Black's telegram says he might be an officer of something called the Great Western Detective League. Ever hear of it?"

Davis shrugged.

"Me neither. He's got some interest in

Gates though."

"Gates gets too close to home. Sounds like we need to deal with both Gates and Shaw."

"Jack needs more men. Keep the checkbook handy. I'm going to tell him to hire them."

"Hope we get more for our money than we got with Dorn. Fact is we've got damn little to show for the time and money we've put into our Johnson County problem."

"You're right about that."

"We keep pushing the rope uphill, hopin' for a different result."

"You got another idea?"

"Put pressure on somebody who don't have some detective at their back."

"Still have to deal with Shaw."

Buffalo

Black put out the word. He was hiring competent men. He made the rounds of the saloons, recruiting. Cane smelled trouble. Black had a half-dozen guns in a couple of days. The night before Black announced they were ready to ride, Briscoe had seen enough. He slipped away for a visit with Sheriff Whitaker.

"What can I do for you?"

"Name's Briscoe Cane. I work with Beau

194

Longstreet. I've been working undercover as a detective for the Stock Growers Association."

"Coming here ain't exactly undercover."

"Time for me to come out in the open. Black's recruited a gang to terrorize small ranchers."

"Where do you figure they plan to strike?"

"I don't know, but I'm pretty sure Dan Shaw's place will be on the list. I'm headed out there to warn Beau."

"What do you want me to do?"

"Wish I knew, Sheriff. Have a posse ready to ride. I'll let you know as soon as I know anything."

Cane rode out toward the Shaw place just after dark. As he rode north on Main Street, he spotted Yankee out front at Maddie's. He wheeled west and stepped down. He clumped up the porch steps and knocked. Longstreet answered the door.

"Trouble?"

Cane nodded, stepping inside. "Black's hired himself gun help."

"How many?"

"Six I know of. I come out to even the odds some."

"Still may need some help."

"Sheriff Whitaker is working on a posse."

"We best get out to the ranch. Maddie,

can we bring Susan here to get her out of trouble's way?"

"Of course. Oh, Beau, will this never end?"

"With Whitaker on the way, we should have Black dead to rights. That should slow things down."

"You be careful."

Cane stepped outside, leaving Beau and Maddie to their moment.

Beau took her in his arms and let her hold tight.

"I'm sorry I worry so. I know you say I shouldn't, but I can't help it."

Beau lifted her chin on thumb and forefinger. "Then I shall just have to love you for it."

He kissed her.

"I'll try."

"It'll be fine."

Shaw Ranch

Clouds banked behind the Big Horns in the west. Wind stiffened, swirling dust devils along the corral. Dan bundled Susan onto the buckboard for the ride to Maddie's over her objections. All three men agreed she needed to seek safe shelter. Longstreet and Cane set to the problem of putting up a defense. They stood in the yard splashed in moonlight.

Longstreet cut his eyes from cabin to barn. "Cabin and barn give us a cross fire."

"Barn loft gives us high cover."

"Dan and I take the cabin; you take the barn?"

"You take the cabin. Dan and I take the barn. That way we maintain cover from both positions, if I slip out the back with some of my friends."

"You brought friends?"

"Did."

"Like it."

"What friends?" Dan asked.

"Little red sticks."

"Dynamite?"

Cane patted his saddlebag and slung it over his shoulder. "Let's go."

Pendleton Ranch

Will Pendleton and his wife, Mary, thought they'd put their troubles behind them with Will's acquittal on rustling charges. Stillness carried for miles on a quiet night at the ranch. Will smoked his pipe while Mary repaired a tear in one of his shirts.

Will cocked an ear. *Riders comin'.* He pulled a Winchester down from its wall mounts over the cabin door and cracked the door. A half-dozen riders sat silhouette in the ranch yard.

"Drop the rifle, Pendleton."

"Who says?"

"I say. Drop it and step outside with the little lady and nobody gets hurt. Light 'em up boys."

Torches flared to light.

"Count 'em Pendleton. One for the barn. Two for the cabin. Get out now before we burn the place down around your ears."

Pendleton glanced back at Mary. Terror lined her face. She came to him. He tossed his rifle clear of the cabin and led her out to the yard.

"You won't get away with this."

"Who's gonna stop us? Torch it, boys."

One rider peeled away to the barn. His torch arced upward, trailing a tail of sparks into the hayloft. Dry tinder exploded in a crown of fire. The other riders rode forward. The first tossed his torch through the open front door. The second threw his on the roof.

"Tell your neighbors, Pendleton. This is what happens to squatters on open range."

"You'll pay for this, Black."

"Not likely." Black's gun blossomed powder flash twice. Will Pendleton slumped to his knees. Mary screamed. Black shot her too. "Come on, boys. Let's get the hell out of here."

Shaw Ranch

"Don't like the looks of that." Dan lifted his chin to a red glow on the eastern horizon.

"What do you make of it?" Beau said.

"I'd say it's the Pendleton place."

"Let's go have a look. If it's what Dan says it is, Briscoe, it might be time for the sheriff to raise that posse."

Pendleton Ranch

The fire continued to rage as Longstreet led them into the yard just as the barn roof collapsed in a shower of sparks. The bodies lay cold in the yard bathed in firelight.

"Stakes is goin' up," Briscoe said.

"They are." Beau stepped down. "Nothing we can do for these poor folks. Briscoe, seems like you should pay the sheriff a visit. Dan and I'll head back to the ranch. I'd bet a month's pay we're next. We'll need help. Have him send someone out here to look after the dead."

Sheriff's Office
Buffalo

Cane found Sheriff Whitaker at his desk by the light of a single lamp, having just finished his nightly rounds. He read Cane's expression.

"Trouble?"

"Yeah. Somebody killed Will Pendleton and his wife. Torched the place. Beau and I figure Dan Shaw is next. We're gonna need help defending the place. I'm hoping you can raise a posse to back us up."

"I'll do best I can."

"Thanks, Sheriff. Beau said we could count on you."

Shaw Ranch

Sun rose, slanting across the deserted yard. Longstreet sipped coffee in the cabin. His Winchester propped against the wall beside the front door. One Colt rode his hip. A second lay on a table beside the window. A box of .44 cartridges at each station.

Dan stood in the shadow beside the loft door, eyes peeled on the rode up from town. A Winchester and double-barreled shotgun propped against the wall where he stood. Cane sat in straw, measuring, cutting, and fixing fuses. His Henry lay atop his crossed legs, a cloud of dust motes rising in the golden glow.

Time passed. Sun climbed to midmorning.

"Here they come!" Dan called.

Longstreet cracked the front door, levered

the Winchester action, chambering a round.

Cane set his saddlebags aside, jacking a Henry round ready.

A distant dun cloud rose on the road from town, a dark knot of horses and riders beneath the spreading haze. They closed to a range of fifty yards. Black drew a halt. One of the men lit a torch. Cane dropped his Henry on a firing line. Then thought better of it. *Best they don't know we're up here right off.*

"Beau."

"Yeah?"

"Can you take the torch?"

"Yeah, if he makes a move."

The torch man wheeled away from the group, angling for the back of the barn.

Longstreet's Winchester cracked. The rider pitched from the saddle, landing on the torch for good measure. His horse galloped away from the flaming screams.

The gang scattered, raining pistol and rifle fire on the cabin. One by one they dropped into pockets of cover. A tree here, a boulder there, another nearby, a shallow ravine wide enough for two on the right. Shooting ceased.

"Give it up, Shaw."

The voice, tree on the left, has to be Black. Cane looked for a shot.

"You and the little woman give it up and ride out of here. Nobody gets hurt. You fight it out we burn you out sure."

Longstreet's answer gouged a chunk of bark from the tree, answered by another volley of return fire. Matters settled into a standoff. Little disturbed the scene save flies buzzing the barn and corral yard.

Cross talk made its way from Black's tree to the boulders to the ravine.

"Something's up," Cane said. "Step back in the shadows, Dan, and change places with me. I want a different firing line."

Quietly they changed places, giving Cane a good line of fire on the ravine.

On Black's next shot, the line erupted in powder smoke. The man at the far-right edge of the ravine bolted for the back of the barn. Cane's shot brought him down.

"The loft!" Someone shouted.

"Down, Dan!"

Bullets pelted the barn wood, ripping holes in the siding and whining through the loft doors.

When the shooting died down, Cane noticed the man at the boulder nearest the ravine must have taken the downed man's place. He produced an unlit torch, holding it away from himself, preparing to light it.

Cane took careful aim. The coal oil—

soaked rags padding the business end of the torch shattered, wrenching the torch from the man's hand.

Another firestorm poured into the loft to no good effect. Shooting died down to another standoff. Time passed. The sun climbed past midday.

"You're askin' for it, Shaw. If I was you, I'd take better care of the little woman than risk getting her killed or roasted alive."

"You mean like Will and Mary Pendleton. You'll never get away with this, Black."

"That's what Pendleton said. He found out dead men tell no tales. Same as you're about to find out."

"I don't think so, Black. A crooked stock detective is too stupid to pull it off." The insult earned Longstreet another volley of fire.

"Atta boy, Black. Burn your ammunition." The truth of that last settled into more standoff.

Sun crossed into late afternoon. Dark clouds poured over the ragged line of Big Horn peaks in the west, rolling across the prairie, riding a gusty wind.

"Looks like we might see some weather," Dan said from the shadows.

"Could."

"Think it might run 'em off?"

"Be a shame if it did before the sheriff gets here. Better we settle something out of this."

Wind shifted out of the northwest.

"Look there," Dan said, his chin lifted to the road from town. Another dun haze rose in the distance, growing at a good pace. "Reinforcements?"

"More likely Sheriff Whitaker and his posse. We've got two in the ravine on the right. One at the first boulder on the left and likely Black behind the tree on the far left. Keep an eye on 'em, Dan. Time for my friends to go to work."

Cane drew double-wrapped dynamite sticks from his saddlebag and lit a cheroot. "Watch." He disappeared at the back of the barn. Down a loft ladder to the corral gate he rounded the side corner and eased his way down the west wall. From there he had a good look as Whitaker and his posse rode in. He lit his fuse, rounded the barn, and threw into the ravine, ducking back behind the barn.

The explosion threw the attackers into complete disarray. One man made it out of the ravine as the sheriff and his men fought to control mounts spooked by the explosion. In the confusion Black and what was left of his men ran for their horses. Some in the posse got off a few shots. The man who escaped the ravine went down. Longstreet picked off the man fleeing the first boulder. When the smoke cleared and the horses settled, everyone was accounted for. Everyone except Black.

"Fan out, boys. See if you can pick up a line on him." Whitaker stepped down.

Longstreet emerged from the cabin. Cane came around the back of the barn. Dan exited, barn door shadow in bright sunlight just as clouds rolled in, eclipsing the light.

"By the look of things, not sure you boys needed us."

"Much obliged, Sheriff," Longstreet said.

Whitaker turned to Cane. "You throw quite a party."

"Comes in handy when the odds tip the wrong way."

"I guess so. Best I get out there with my men to see if anyone's got a trail. I'll send someone out to do the undertaking." He hauled himself back in the saddle, touched the brim of his hat, and rode out.

Black cut his horse up a narrow rocky draw and stepped down. He reloaded his pistol and waited. One of the possemen passed him by. *Son of a bitch! That was close. Dynamite explains a lot. Maybe even Dorn.*

The kill list keeps getting longer. Better concentrate on the one can't get away 'til we figure out what to do about the rest of these snakes.

CHAPTER TWENTY-ONE

O'Rourke House
1911

"Hello, Robert." Angela brushed an errant gray tendril behind her ear. "Come in, come in. Saturday already. Where do the weeks go? Did you have any luck at Ethel's estate sale?"

"We purchased a settee Penny thought quite lovely."

"And a bargain I'm sure."

"Bargain on our budget is not such a lofty subject. I am told we saved sixty dollars off the catalog price for new. Still the savings came at a price dear to me."

"One never regrets the purchase of fine furnishings."

"Regret, I suppose not, but one is left to wonder where a kitchen set might be found."

"In the kitchen," Briscoe said stepping off the stairs."

"Robert was discussing the wherewithal to purchase a kitchen set after investing in a settee, dear."

"Sell more books. Shall we begin?"

"The man has an answer for everything."

"I've noticed."

Briscoe led the way to the parlor and took his customary seat. "Now, where were we?"

I consulted my notes. "Your dynamite and a sheriff's posse ended a standoff at the Shaw Ranch. Unfortunately, Black made his escape."

"Ah yes, Black. All those possemen fanned out looking and still they lost him. Things got quiet for a spell after that, though as you might expect we hadn't heard the last of a varmint like Jack Black . . ."

Hart Street

Supper ended, Maddie nestled in Beau's arm on the porch swing as day disappeared in the lengthening shadows of evening.

"Do you suppose that could be the end of it?"

"I'd like to think so, but I doubt it. The cattle barons have too much at stake in their view. They've got nothing to show for all their trouble. The ranchers and settlers are still here."

"Not the Pendletons."

208

"No, not the Pendletons."

"What will they do next?"

"That, my dear, is the question of the hour. If we knew the answer to that one, we could take steps to prevent it. My guess is they will have to do something before Gates goes on trial in a few weeks. Dan's testimony will turn the light of the law on the Wyoming Stock Growers Association and those behind the attacks."

"I take it you haven't had any luck getting Gates to cooperate."

"None. He's either convinced he'll get off somehow or he's afraid. Either way he's going to end up taking a fall for whoever is calling the shots in Cheyenne."

"So, you still need to protect Dan and Susan."

"I do."

"There's the silver lining."

"Silver lining?"

"Keeps you nearby."

"If I didn't know better, I might think the lady likes having me around."

"You don't know better."

"That come with a kiss?"

And it did.

"Best I get out to the ranch."

"You should before my resolution goes wobbly or worse."

"Wobbly is it? Now I'm not so sure."

Another kiss.

"Wobbly yet?"

"Worse."

Another, lingering this time.

"Working?"

"Now I'm sure. You need to protect the Shaws and me."

"You?"

"From myself."

"If you say so, but only because I love you and don't want to frighten you off."

"You do frighten me, and I love you for it."

"I declare, Maddie O'Rourke, I shall never figure you out."

She smiled. "Good."

"Good?"

"Keeps you interested."

Shaw Ranch

A week passed, then two, with no sign of Black or anyone else from the Stock Growers Association. Cane kept a low profile in town and in touch with Sheriff Whitaker. Dan met Longstreet in the barn as he did every morning.

"Mornin'."

"Mornin', Dan."

"How much longer you figure you need

to be keepin' an eye on the place? Not that I mind havin' your help. Just can't think I can thank you enough for all you done."

"Wish I knew. At least until Gates goes on trial."

"Any idea when that might be?"

"Briscoe says the circuit judge is due in town in the next week or two."

"Can't get here soon enough for me."

"Gates is nothing more than a foot soldier. Your testimony will put him away. Sheriff Whitaker and I keep pressuring him on how big a fall he is willing to take for the likes of his handlers. You'd think at some point he'd take a deal to get leniency for himself. We really won't have this thing licked until we get to the cattle barons behind it in a meaningful way."

"You figure you can?"

"Don't know. The rich and powerful don't go down easy. Squeeze 'em hard enough and you never know what they might do."

"From what we've seen so far, they're capable of most anything."

"Seems so. Tough to prepare for that."

Cattlemen's Club
Cheyenne, Wyoming Territory
McGant and Chesterfield sat in the high-

stakes game room wreathed in a blue cigar haze.

"What are we gonna do, Buck? Gates is goin' to trial in a week or two and Shaw is still drawing breath."

"It's a problem. Black's on his own. None of what's left of the local gunnies will have anything to do with him after the way the attack on the Shaw place got shot all to hell. Dynamite is scary shit."

"Gates goes to trial and Shaw testifies, matters get ugly for us; and we're still starin' at a county full of open range squatters."

"Two problems, Davis. Ain't one answer for both." McGant topped up their glasses.

"Well we better fix the Shaw problem fast. That one's got a calendar runnin' against us."

"We haven't had much luck with the Shaw part of the problem. That leaves one part, Black may be able to fix."

"What's that?"

"Gates."

Sheriff's Office
Buffalo

Black slipped into the darkened alley behind the jail. Buffalo stood dead silent and still in the small hours of night with even the saloons having gone mostly quiet. He made his way along the back wall, pausing now and again to look and listen, making sure he was alone. He reached the barred window to Gates's cell. Soft snores rose and fell in rhythmic breathing.

"Rusty," he hushed.

Nothing.

He drew his gun and tapped the barrel on a bar.

"Who's there?"

"It's me, Jack."

Gates's face appeared in shadow at the bars. "What's up?"

"You alone?"

"Sheriff's gone for the night. I'm his only guest if that's what you mean."

"Good. I'm gonna get you out of there."

"How?"

"Pull out the bars."

"How the hell you gonna do that?"

"Good stout rope and a strong horse."

"I'm from Missouri, but it's worth a try."

"Slip this around the three middle bars here." Black threaded one end of a rope through the bars. Gates pulled it through and around the third bar.

"What was that?" Black hissed.

"What?"

"I heard something in there."

Gates looked over his shoulder. Black

looped the rope over Gates's head and jerked hard, slamming the back of his head against the bars.

"Ugh!" Gates struggled against the bars, clawing at the rope fighting for life. "Can't brea . . ."

Black held on tight. Tension against the rope eased to dead weight. A few minutes more and shit smell proclaimed the work complete. He let go of the rope, releasing the body to the floor.

Paradise Saloon
Black peered over the batwings. *Paradise, some name for this dump.* The bartender snored at one end of the bar. His only customer slumped over a corner table, exactly where Black expected to find him. He slipped inside, approaching the drunk's table. He pulled up a chair and nudged the disheveled dissipated remains.

"Wake up, Cady," he hissed.

"Leave me alone."

"We got business to discuss."

"Go away."

"I got a job for you."

"Not interested."

"Pays fifty dollars."

A red-rimmed watery eye cracked. "Doin' what?"

CHAPTER TWENTY-TWO

Cheyenne Leader
Stock Detective Murdered in Johnson County Jail
Star witness and others angered law
didn't go far enough fast enough.
Sheriff complicit in rustler revenge.

Cattlemen's Club

The high-stakes card room had the feel of a more relaxed atmosphere for the evening. "That settles problem one," Chesterfield said, lifting his glass in toast.

"Better than settles." McGant took a swallow.

"What do you mean?"

"Black bought himself a town drunk who'll swear he saw Dan Shaw leave the scene that night."

"I was beginning to lose faith in Jack. Looks like he finally got this one right."

"Does."

"I'll drink to that."

McGant topped up their glasses.

"Now what's to be done about our county full of squatters?"

"I've given that some thought."

"And?"

"It'll take some time and comes at a high price."

"What doesn't these days. What have you got in mind this time?"

"We're gonna raise us an army."

"An army?"

"Take one to invade Johnson County."

"Invade Johnson County?"

"Root out and burn out every last man Jack and Jenny of 'em."

"You're talkin' range war, Buck."

"If that's what it takes. I'll put the word out. You get the bank balance limbered up."

Shaw Ranch

Sheriff Ben Whitaker rode into the yard under bright midday sun and stepped down. Susan answered his knock at the cabin door.

"Sheriff Whitaker, what a pleasant surprise."

"Morning, Mrs. Shaw. I'm afraid it's not a social call. Is Dan about?"

"He's in the barn. Is something wrong?"

"I've a warrant to serve."

Alarmed, Susan followed him to the barn.

Dan crouched beside a bucket of grease, brushing the buckboard axle.

"Sheriff Whitaker, what can I do for you?"

"Sorry to say, Dan, you're under arrest."

He dropped the brush in the bucket. "Arrest for what?"

"For the murder of Red Gates."

"Gates is dead?"

"Found strangled in his cell two days ago."

"What makes you think I had anything to do with it?"

"Cady Yates swears he saw you leave the alley behind the jail the night of the murder."

"Cady Yates hasn't drawn a sober breath in years. You call that a reliable witness? He's wrong. I was right here where I belong two nights ago. Ask Susan."

"He was, Sheriff."

"That'll be for a jury to decide. For now, I gotta take you in, Dan."

"You know this is a stock growers' setup."

"Not sayin' that's not a possibility. Cheyenne papers is sayin' I'm complicit in Gates's death. I got no choice but to take you in."

"Cheyenne papers would. You know they're in the growers' pocket. Never printed a truthful word where Johnson

County is concerned. No reason to believe any of it now."

"Sorry, Dan. Best saddle a horse."

Hart Street

The sound of a wagon clattering to a halt at her gate drew Maddie to the window curtain. An anxious looking Susan Shaw stepped down from her buckboard and started up the walk. Maddie went to the door.

"Is Mr. Longstreet here?"

"Haven't seen him since he left for your place last night. Is something wrong?"

"Oh, Maddie, they've arrested Dan."

"Arrested Dan? What on earth for?"

"The murder of Red Gates."

"Murder? Here, come inside."

"It's not true of course. Cady Yates made the accusation. Sheriff Whitaker said he had no choice but to lock Dan up."

"And Beau wasn't there?" Maddie closed the door.

"He left early this morning. Didn't say where he was going. I thought he might have come here."

"Only thing I can think is he might have gone into town to see Briscoe. We can take your buckboard into town to look for them."

"I'm so scared. Gates was murdered in

his jail cell. The jail's not safe. We know the cattle growers want Dan dead."

At that a horse and rider sounded out front. Maddie turned to the door.

"It's Beau." She opened the door as he hurried up the walk.

"Gates is dead," he said.

"We know. Susan tells me Sheriff Whitaker arrested Dan for the murder."

"Dan? What makes Ben think Dan had anything to do with it?"

"Cady Yates accused him," Susan said.

"Who's Cady Yates?"

"A person of low character."

"Town drunk, some would say," Maddie added.

"I'm so frightened for Dan. The jail's not safe. Gates was killed in his cell."

"I know. Briscoe told me. Don't worry, Susan. We'll get him out of there. In the meantime, I want you to stay here with Maddie. I'll be by when it's safe to go home."

"You think they might do something to the ranch?"

"All I know is these people are capable of anything. We're not gonna take any chances."

He gave Maddie a hug and was gone.

Longstreet tied up a lathered Yankee at the hitch rack right beside Smoke. *Good. No need to go lookin' for Briscoe.* Whitaker sat at his desk.

"Longstreet, glad you're here."

"I understand you've arrested Dan Shaw."

"He has," Cane said. "I came as soon as I heard."

"Glad you did. I been thinkin' on my way into town how to play this. Gates was murdered to keep his case from going to trial when the big boys down south had no luck getting rid of Dan. Dan is a sitting duck in here. We need to get him out and get him out fast."

"I can't just let him go. Papers is already claimin' I'm complicit in the killin' some way."

"Who's this Cady Yates?"

"Town drunk."

"So I hear. Where do we find him?"

"When he's not in here, Paradise Saloon on south Main. Be there toward evenin' after he sleeps off last night."

"Paradise?"

"Owner fancies himself a sense of humor."

"Alright. It's likely he's been paid to make this charge. Probably by Black before he crawled into whatever hole he's hid out in. Yates most likely doesn't know you've resigned from the stock detective services, Briscoe. You'd be the one to tease the truth out of him."

Briscoe nodded. "What's this feller look like?"

"Ask the bartender. They all know him."

"Why didn't I think of that."

"Meantime, Sheriff, if you don't mind, I'm going to stand guard by Dan."

"I'd like to say that won't be necessary, but I've been wrong about that before."

CHAPTER TWENTY-THREE

O'Rourke House
Denver
1911

Angela answered my knock on a rainy overcast Saturday afternoon.

"Robert, I'm so glad you're here. I've something to show you. Come along. I remembered it after you left last week."

"I thought the young man was here to see me." Briscoe rose in the parlor.

"He is, dear. This won't take long. Come along if you like."

Mystified, I followed Angela through the kitchen, out the back door, and down the steps to a walkway leading to a carriage house. The door swung open with a groan as we made our way into the dim interior. She led the way to the back of a cavernous barn and a room likely once having served as a tack room. She opened the door to a dusty assortment of nondescript disused and discarded implements, jars, jugs, barrels, and crates, gray lit by a single rain-spattered window.

"There," she pointed to a tarp in a dark corner. She pulled the tarp away, revealing a kitchen set in sad need of refurbishing. "It's sound. Good wood. Needs refinishing, but here's the best part: it's yours for the taking."

I looked closer. I winced within myself, uncertain what to say. The set, apart from its condition, was identical to the set in Mrs. David's estate sale. The one Penny misliked.

"Why this is so generous. It's only I know nothing of furniture refinishing."

Briscoe bent over the table, sweeping a hand over the surface. "Golden oak unless I miss my guess. Should finish up right fancy with a little elbow grease."

"Elbow grease?"

"Just an expression. Something you become familiar with as a homeowner."

"Homeowner," Angela declared hands on hips. "What would you know of home ownership?"

"I am a trained observer."

"I should have known as much. I've been the subject of much of it."

"Pleasantly so."

"In whose estimation?"

"Now about refinishing this table and chairs, Robert, there's really nothing to it. I can coach you through it."

"Supervising work is one of Briscoe's specialties. I can attest."

Trapped, I couldn't very well refuse the kindness. Beggars best not indeed be choosers and for a practical matter we needed a place to eat. "If you think I can manage it with your help, Briscoe, let's give it a try."

"We'll get started next week. Now let's get back to your book."

Paradise Saloon
Buffalo

Cane pushed through broken batwings. Dim light failed to disguise the dingy condition of the premises. The air hung thick, smelling of stale tobacco smoke, beer, and unwashed bodies. A handful of customers scattered about. Cane approached a bartender wearing an apron that may have been white some years ago.

"What can I do for you?"

"Lookin' for Cady Yates."

"That's him." He thumbed a dark figure hunched over a table, a bottle, and a glass.

He lifted one bloodshot eye at Cane's approach.

"What you want?"

Early, the slur slight.

"Jack Black sent me."

"I done it. I toldt the sheriff."

"You're not done, you know. You're gonna have to tell it to the judge. Jack wants to be sure you do that."

He tossed off his drink and poured another. "Hell, I know that. Ain't stupid, you know."

"You stay in town until the trial. Don't try leavin'. We'll be watchin'. You hear?"

"Ain't goin' nowhere."

"Good."

Sheriff's Office

Cane stopped at the office to check in with Longstreet. He found him outside, seated on a bench wrapped in deep shadow.

"What are you doin' out here?"

"Keeping an eye on the alley. Nobody inside gonna do Dan any harm. You find him?"

"Did."

"Where?"

"Paradise Saloon just like Whitaker said."

"Was it?"

"Paradise? A feller needs to be drunk to stomach that place."

"That good."

"That good."

"Are you?"

"Am I what?"

"Drunk."

"What gives you that idea?"

"Stomached the place, didn't you?"

"Stood it just long enough without the benefit of strong spirits support."

"And?"

"Left him thinkin' I'm with Black. He'll break if we squeeze him. Just need to find the time and place."

"Not in Paradise?"

"Definitely not in Paradise." Cane yawned. "I'm gonna turn in. You want me to spell you later?"

"Get some rest. I'll grab a cell bunk at first light."

Night crawled to quiet in the small hours. Longstreet's thoughts drifted. *Maddie. Now what?* What's fair? He said he'd changed. He felt it. Did felt it mean live it? Then there is the practical problem. Give up the league and what do you do to make a living? You're no rancher. Farmer? Not a chance. Shopkeeper? Boredom be fatal. Still there's Maddie. Feels as needful as breathing now, having her back.

A soft scrape down the boardwalk brought him alert. A glimpse of shadow disappeared in alley darkness. Longstreet drew his pocket pistol from its shoulder rig, eased off the bench, and followed down the alley. Pale moonlight washed the back of the jail. A man moved in silhouette along the wall, pausing to listen at the first cell window. He moved on to the second. Dan's window. Moonlight caught the glint of a gun.

"Drop it!" Beau punctuated the command, cocking his gun.

Black spun low, snapping off a quick shot in blinding muzzle flash; the bullet ricocheted off the jail wall beside Longstreet's left shoulder.

Longstreet fired into the muzzle flash twice, dropping the stock detective to his knees. He pitched forward on his face and lay still.

"Beau, is that you?"

"It's alright, Dan. This one won't bother us anymore."

Gunplay in the middle of the night brings out the best in civic duty. It was no more than a few minutes before a sleep-disheveled Sheriff Whitaker rounded the wall to the jail back alley.

"What happened?"

"Evenin', Ben."

"That who I think it is?"

"Is."

"Well you called that one, Beau. Can't say I'm surprised. Glad you were here. Dan alright?"

"Fine, Sheriff," came a voice behind the cell bars. "Thanks to Beau here again."

"We'll be needin' the undertaker," Longstreet said.

"I'll take care of it. Cane have any luck with Yates?"

"Briscoe says he'll break when we squeeze."

Whitaker tossed his head at Black's remains. "Might be just the squeeze we need."

"Might at that."

Paradise Saloon

Cane swung through the broken batwings. If the place was a dump in the dark, it turned fit for a pigsty in morning light. The bartender dozed on a stool at one end of the bar.

"Where's Yates?"

He blinked awake. "Sleepin' it off. Upstairs, first door on the right."

The stairs groaned. The second floor added the aroma of chamber pot to stale beer, tobacco, and unwashed humanity. Cane opened the door to what must have once been a whore's crib when Paradise was

228

prosperous enough to employ soiled doves. Yates sprawled on a stained mattress, mouth agape.

Cane prodded him with the toe of his boot. "Wake up!"

Yates roused with a guttural protest and retched. "You. What you want now?"

"Black's dead."

"Dead?"

"Dead."

"What's that to me? I done what he said."

"Here's what it means to you, trouble. See, I saw you leave the scene of his killing last night."

"You saw no such thing. I had nothin' to do with it."

"I say you did. That's what I'm tellin' the sheriff."

"That's a lie."

"So is the lie you told the sheriff about Dan Shaw. The lie Black paid you to tell. So, here's the deal: we march down to the jail now and you tell the sheriff you lied, or I tell him you killed Black. Since you say you ain't stupid, you likely know murder's a hangin' offense. Now what's it gonna be?"

"I'll tell him. Though hangin' might be a relief to this hangover."

CHAPTER TWENTY-FOUR

Hart Street

Dan and Longstreet tied up at Maddie's gate. Both were greeted by relieved hugs.

"What happened?" Susan asked.

"Black's dead. Beau here dropped him last night. Briscoe persuaded Yates to admit Black paid him to lie. Sheriff Whitaker dropped the charges."

"That's all good news. Where does that leave us?"

"On our way home. I'll hitch up the buckboard." Dan left.

"Maddie, I can't thank you enough for letting me stay with you through all of this. It made things so much easier."

"Happy to help, Susan." They exchanged a hug.

"And thank you for all you've done for us, Beau. I hate to think what might have happened to Dan if you hadn't been watching over him."

"You go along home and take care of each other."

Susan went out to the yard as Dan finished harnessing the mule.

Maddie closed the door and turned into Beau's arms. They held each other for a time.

"Come and sit." She led him to the parlor settee.

They sat together, his arm around her.

"Is it over?"

"For the moment. Long term, I doubt it."

"What will you do now?"

"Stay close."

"I like the sound of that."

"Glad you do."

"Beau, I've been thinking."

"Don't."

"Don't think?"

"Not now. Not yet. Let time tell us."

"Will it?"

"I think it will."

"Now who's thinking?"

"I am. Good thoughts too. For the time being, let's just let us be."

"If you say so. There I go again. What's happening to me?"

"Some might call it love."

"Hmm," she snuggled closer.

Cheyenne Leader
Stock Detective Killed in Jailhouse Shootout
Johnson County Justice Frees Accused Stock Detective Murderer

Wyoming Stock Growers Association stock detective Jack Black was gunned down in Johnson County by an unnamed assailant in a shootout at the Buffalo jailhouse. In a related matter, charges against rancher Dan Shaw, accused in the jailhouse killing of WSGA stock detective Red Gates, were dropped when a witness to the case withdrew his accusation. Shaw was subsequently released. These developments beg the question, what are the good people of Wyoming to expect when it comes to law and order in Johnson County? At what point does it become necessary for the governor to restore order in a renegade county?

Seth Adams folded the paper. *Tinder-dry field, waitin' for a match.* Best keep an eye on them holdin' the lucifers.

Cattlemen's Club
McGant paced the game room, fuming. Chesterfield watched, expecting spontane-

232

ous conflagration at any moment.

"Black's dead. Powder River range is still overrun with rats."

"How's your army coming along?"

"Word's out. We should start seeing takers any day now. What's the treasury look like?"

"We're healed."

"We better be. It's gonna be expensive."

"Do you think we should whisper in Governor Barber's ear? Just a courtesy to let him know what's coming."

"You're on good terms with him, aren't you."

"Amos and I get together for cards now and again."

"Couldn't hurt, could it."

"I'll get to it."

Governor's Office
Cheyenne

Wyoming Governor Amos Barber sat at an imposing desk in a spacious office set atop capitol hill. Morning sun streamed through a pair of floor-to-ceiling windows. A copy of the *Cheyenne Daily Leader* lay at his elbow. The lead story called to question the role of his office and territorial government concerning the situation in Johnson County. It was a question to ponder. One he knew to be important to the interests of his wealthiest constituents, constituents essential to his holding the office he occupied. The office door opened, interrupting his train of thought.

"Davis Chesterfield is here to see you, sir."

Speaking of wealthy constituents concerned with the Johnson County problem. "Send him in, Thomas. And bring us both a cup of coffee if you would."

"Very good, sir."

Barber rose to greet his visitor.

"Good morning, Davis. Pleasant surprise seeing you in daylight. Don't suppose you came looking for a game."

"Thanks for seeing me unannounced, Amos, and no, I didn't come looking for a game." He nodded to the newspaper on the governor's desk. "I suspect you can guess why I'm here."

"Have a seat."

Thomas appeared with two steaming cups of coffee he placed on the desk.

"Thank you, Thomas. Close the door on your way out."

"Now Davis, what's on your mind?"

"The situation in Johnson County has grown intolerable. Rustling is rampant. Local law is unable or unwilling to enforce order and when our detectives make arrests the courts turn the criminals loose. Recently we've had two stock detectives murdered, as you read in that paper."

"I understand your concern, though I'm at something of a loss as to know what to do about it. The territory lacks law enforcement resources. I could make a request of the U.S. Marshal's service, but I believe they would balk on grounds of jurisdiction."

"I see you've given the matter some thought. Thank you for that. We understand the limitations you face. We on the other hand are not so limited."

"I'm listening."

"Consider this a courtesy call, Amos. The Wyoming Stock Growers Association is recruiting a sizable number of stock detectives to address the situation in Johnson County."

"How sizable?"

"Sizable enough to do the job."

"Sounds like an invasion."

"Your word. I wouldn't use it if I were you."

"What is it you want me to do then?"

"Nothing. Leave matters to us."

"What if you encounter resistance?"

"We intend to act with overwhelming force."

"I assume you and Buck know what you are doing. Appearances may make the politics dicey. You know you can count on this office to be supportive, albeit passively."

"We understand and that's perfect."

"I appreciate the courtesy of your warning. I presume you will keep matters on the right side of the law."

"Rest assured we will be acting to protect our rightful property rights. Anything beyond that would be the doing of others."

It started as a trickle, Deputy Adams noted on his rounds. Strangers drifting into town. Hard men. Heavily armed. Days passed. They came by horse. They came by rail. They came from the west, the south, and the east. A dozen, then two, fifty and more. They had the makings of a small army.

Nosing around the saloons, Seth picked up gossip. Word was Wyoming Stock Growers Association was hiring. *Tinder-dry field.* There's a load of trouble headed Mr. Longstreet's way. Be willin' to bet a month's pay on that.

Sheriff's Office
Buffalo

The young lad who ran telegrams for Western Union swung through the office door. He handed Sheriff Whitaker an envelope addressed Beau Longstreet c/o sheriff's office, Buffalo, Wyoming Territory. Telegrams came with their own stamp of urgency. Whitaker put on his hat and headed for the livery stable to collect his horse.

Shaw Ranch
Sheriff Whitaker rode into the yard under a gray cloud deck shedding light rain.

Now what, Dan thought. "Afternoon, Sheriff."

Whitaker stepped down. "Afternoon, Dan. Longstreet around?"

Beau stepped out of the barn. "What can I do for you, Sheriff?"

"Got a telegram for you. Came in this morning. Thought I'd best get it out to you pronto." He fished it out of his vest pocket and handed it over.

Longstreet tore it open.

Cheyenne
Cattle growers hiring gunmen stop. Something over fifty now stop. Coming for Johnson
County stop.
Seth

Longstreet handed the telegram back to Whitaker. "Have a look."

Whitaker read. "Who's Seth?"

237

"Deputy sheriff in Cheyenne."

"What's up?" Dan asked.

Longstreet handed him the telegram.

He glanced from Longstreet to Whitaker. "What are we going to do?"

"Sheriff?" Longstreet said.

"Get ready for war."

"Afraid so. Briscoe and I can work on the welcome, Sheriff. You and Dan need to get the word out. We'll likely need every able-bodied man deputized to meet this threat."

Heads nodded.

"Let's get to it."

O'Rourke House
Denver
1911

We changed our weekly routine, shortening our time working on the book to allow time in the carriage house to work on refinishing the kitchen set. Briscoe showed me how to remove the old finish using sandpaper. Coarse grade at first, fine grade to finish. It proved a long, slow process. Ornate spindles on the table and chair legs took time and care to preserve. Gradually, beautiful oak grain emerged in the wood.

"Comin' right along," Briscoe said.

"Is."

"Time to think about the color stain you

plan to use."

"I've no idea. What do you think?"

"If it was me, with this oak grain I'd go with a golden oak stain."

"Oh, this is coming along nicely," Angela said as she entered the carriage house back-room.

"We were just discussing stains," I said. "Have you any thoughts on that?"

"Mmm, fine grain. I think I might favor a darker walnut. That would be very rich."

Now where to? I've a set Penny doesn't prefer, and I have to guess at a stain. "How do I decide?"

"Hardware store sells paint. They'll have stain samples. Might as well get to know the hardware store. As a homeowner, you'll be spending more time there than you might imagine."

"Sound advice," Angela said.

"Did you hear that, Robert? Sound advice, she said."

"Don't let the rarity go to your head."

"Still sound."

"Fair enough. Now let's get back to writing. I know something about that."

CHAPTER TWENTY-FIVE

Cheyenne Station
Union Pacific made up a special train to take them as far as Casper. They needed four stock cars just for the horses. McGant and Chesterfield supervised the loading. Deputy Seth Adams squinted into the morning sun across Hill Street from the depot. Fifty men, all armed with long guns and one or more sidearms. *They's a storm headed Buffalo way.* Best let Longstreet know. He crossed Hill to the Western Union office in the depot.

Sheriff's Office
Buffalo

> *Cheyenne*
> *WSGA force entrain for Casper stop.*
> *Fifty men stop. Good luck stop.*
> *Seth*

Longstreet handed the telegram to Cane.

240

Cane passed the foolscap to Whitaker. "What do you figure, six days?" Cane asked. "Likely," Beau said. "Time enough to arrange a warm welcome."

"What do you have in mind?" Whitaker handed the telegram back to Beau.

"We set up a target to tip them off to. Lure them into a trap. Get them engaged and then hit them with the biggest posse we can raise. Any ideas where we might set them up, Sheriff?"

Whitaker turned to a map of Johnson County on the office wall. He ran his finger southwest from Buffalo.

"Nate Champion's N Bar C Ranch is here. Nate's been under as much pressure as anybody. Neighboring ranch to the southeast, MC Ranch, is owned by Buck McGant. He's one of the more influential cattle barons. The stock growers ain't doin' nothin' he ain't in on. Nate'll be smack in harm's way of what's comin'. I'm guessin' he'll throw in on this plan."

"Alright, here's what we do, Sheriff. You and I ride down there to talk to Champion. I'll stay there to help organize the defenses once he's signed on. Sheriff, you ride on from there to raise a posse from the ranches and farms east and north. Briscoe, ride out to the Shaw place. Have Dan recruit posse members from settlers to the west and south. Have them meet the sheriff in Buffalo in four days. Then come on down to N Bar C Ranch. You can help me with our defenses. Oh, and bring along some of your favorite toys."

"Already had them on my shopping list, along with extra ammunition."

"Good. Let's ride."

Shaw Ranch
Cane loped Smoke into the ranch yard and swung down. Dan stepped out of the barn wiping his hands on a rag.

"Afternoon, Mr. Cane. What can I do for you?"

"Trouble's coming, Dan."

"Not again."

"Afraid so. The stock growers got a force of fifty gunmen headed this way. We've got five, maybe six days to prepare to face them."

"What do we do?"

"Sheriff Whitaker is out raising a posse. A big posse. He needs your help to work the ranches and farms west and south of here. We need every able-bodied man to meet the sheriff in Buffalo in four days to be deputized."

"I'll spread the word. Count on it."

Cane nodded, swinging into the saddle. He wheeled away south.

Dan started back to the barn.

N Bar C Ranch

Nate Champion bent over a leaky water tank in need of a patch. He glanced north at the sight of two riders cresting a nearby hill. He reached for the Winchester at his side, uncertain of who they might be and what they might want. He relaxed, recognizing Sheriff Whitaker.

The riders drew rein.

"Afternoon, Nate." Whitaker and Longstreet stepped down.

"Afternoon, Sheriff. To what do I owe the pleasure?"

"Trouble, I'm afraid. This here's Beau Longstreet. He's been helpin' Dan Shaw with his cattle grower problems."

"Heard some about that. Pleased to meet you, Mr. Longstreet."

"I'll let Beau tell you what we're up against."

"Cattle growers are coming this way in force. Fifty guns is what we hear. Sheriff thinks your place will be front and center at the start of trouble."

"Likely so. Question is, what can I do against a force the size of that?"

"The answer is what we do against a force the size of that. If you're willing, we have a plan."

"Willing? Don't look like I have much choice. What's the plan?"

"We bait them into a trap. My partner is on his way here. The three of us will organize a defense of your ranch. The sheriff is in the process of raising a big posse."

"Every able-bodied hand in the county, I'll wager," Whitaker said.

"We'll arrange a real warm welcome to keep them busy. The sheriff and his posse reverse the odds and we send 'em packin' back where they came from. What do you say?"

"What can I say? Sounds like the best chance we got. Only, Sheriff?"

"Yeah."

"Don't be late."

Whitaker stepped into his saddle. He squeezed up an easy lope northeast.

"Now let's have a look at your ranch quarters."

French Creek

Dan made Joe Peck's ranch on French Creek his first stop. Joe's place was northwest of Dan's, which meant Joe could help in more ways than one. Dan rode in to find

Joe bent over the hind hoof of a sturdy bay mare, tapping a hammer to a shoe. He let the hoof down and took three nails from his mouth by way of greeting.

"Afternoon, Dan. What brings you all the way out here?"

"Helpin' the sheriff raise a posse."

"Now what?"

"Cattle growers got fifty guns headed this way."

"Damn those greedy bastards! Just can't abide we got a right to be here."

"Seems so. Still we need every man with a stake in the county."

"What can I do?"

"I'll head north. If you head south toward town tell everyone you can to meet the sheriff in town to be deputized four days from now."

"I'll ride, soon as I finish this shoe."

"Thanks, Joe. See you in town."

Dan wheeled northwest.

Joe replaced the nails in his mouth and picked up the hoof.

N Bar C Ranch

The ranch headquarters looked defensible. It sat on a rise, surrounded by open prairie, offering good fields of fire with limited cover for would-be attackers. A sturdy log ranch home sat at the bottom, a U, with the sides formed by a barn and corral on the right and a bunkhouse on the left.

"What do you think?" Nate asked.

"I think we can work with this. I'm thinkin' you in the house, me in the bunkhouse, and Briscoe in the barn where he has room to work."

"Briscoe?"

"My partner."

"What sort of work does he do?"

Longstreet smiled. "Magic."

"Magic?"

"With dynamite."

"Like the sound of them odds."

"Three against fifty, we'll need all the odds we can get."

Casper, Wyoming Territory

The Union Pacific charter ground to a halt at end of track, belching black smoke to blue sky, brakes squealed gouts of white steam. McGant and Chesterfield swung down from a caboose outfitted for a private car. Up the line men poured out the passenger cars, while stockmen rolled ramps into place for off-loading the horses. McGant strode up the platform to the knot of men awaiting orders.

"Alright men, listen up. Put your horses

up at the livery. You can enjoy the night in town but be saddled and ready to ride north sunup tomorrow."

The men drifted down the platform to collect their mounts as they were led down the ramps from the stock cars.

"Damn squatters up north is in for a rude awakening from that bunch," Chesterfield said.

"Won't know what the hell hit 'em by the time we flush 'em out. Come on, Davis. Let's see if the hotel has a suite and a decent bottle of whiskey."

"Sounds right about now."

Rock Creek

Sheriff Whitaker splashed across Rock Creek, loping up the road to Ruben Toller's place. He found Toller repairing a broken corral rail.

"Mornin', Sheriff. What brings you by?"

"Raising a posse, Ruben. Need every man we can get. Stock growers is sending a small army this way. Looks like they aim to run us out of the county."

"Sounds serious."

"It is."

"Do we know how much time we got?"

"Five, maybe four days. Men are gathering in town to be deputized four days from now."

"You can count on me, Sheriff."

"Actually, I got a job for you. The cattle growers will be riding north out of Casper. I want you to meet up with them. Tell 'em they'll find what they come for at Nate Champion's N Bar C Ranch."

"Nate know about this?"

"More than knows. We're arranging a little welcome to Johnson County reception for those boys. You're gonna make sure they get their invitation. You can join up with the posse north of N bar C when you're done."

"Happy to oblige, Sheriff."

"Thanks, Ruben. Knew I could count on you." Whitaker wheeled away north.

CHAPTER TWENTY-SIX

Casper

Predawn pink tinged the eastern sky. Soft sounds of men, horses, and saddle leather colored the morning stillness. More than a few of the men moving a little slow after a night in town. McGant toed a stirrup and stepped aboard, signaling the rest to mount. Saddles creaked in waves; horses snorted and stomped. McGant led out in an easy trot as morning sun peeked over the horizon.

The knot of men stretched to an irregular column, stirrup to stirrup, nose to tail, resolute men born on a tide of pounding hooves. Sun rose over the ride to a midday rest stop for hardtack and coffee. North, ever north to waning sun and the onset of purple shadow and a first night's camp.

McGant's band rode north at dawn the second day. They camped on a creek bank the second night. McGant and Chesterfield sat at their campfire polishing off the last of supper on the trail.

"Made good time today," Chesterfield said.

"Did. Reckon we'll make MC day after tomorrow."

"Then what?"

"Then we go huntin'."

N Bar C Ranch

"This'll do," Cane said, assessing Longstreet's plan of defense. "At least as much as anything can do for the prospect of a fight outnumbered fifty to three."

"You got tricks up your sleeve?" Beau asked.

"I might. Let's take a walk."

The walk took in places where prairie terrain might afford attackers cover. These, Briscoe marked with stones.

"What in blazes are you doing?"

"You'll see. This should do it. Time for a little practice."

"Practice?"

"This way."

Cane stalked off to the barn. He pulled his Henry rifle from Smoke's saddle boot along with a long slender implement wrapped in cloth. He threw his saddlebags over his shoulder and climbed into the loft.

Longstreet followed. Low lit by the light of the door, the loft offered the cover of gloom. From the left side of the loft door, Cane had cover and line sight to most of the cover positions he marked out. He unwrapped his package. A long bow and three arrows each with a stick of dynamite lashed behind the tip.

Longstreet's jaw dropped. "You plannin' what I think you're plannin'?"

"What's it look like?"

"Looks like you're fixin' to drop some serious noise on somebody. You think it'll work?"

"We'll know soon enough."

He nocked an arrow, drew, and let fly, testing the arc and counting off seconds until the arrow struck ground short of the target. Two more shots gave him trajectory to the first emplacement.

"Well I'll be . . ." Longstreet said.

"Not if I can help it." Cane spent the rest of the afternoon mapping the remaining rock positions, noting the trajectory to each and seconds to reach the target. He then cut fuses to match targets of opportunity once the festivities started.

Nate watched, amazed. "Does he do this sort of thing often?"

Longstreet shrugged. "Mostly he throws

251

his little bundles of joy. I've never seen the bow and arrow trick before."

"Will it work?"

"Briscoe thinks so. Chances are if it works once, it'll scare the livin' daylights out of those boys."

"Just as long as he doesn't blow us to kingdom come in the bargain."

"I've been around Briscoe's magic a time or two and I'm still here to talk about it. I wouldn't worry too much if I were you."

"If you say so."

Buffalo

They gathered in town, answering a call to common defense. Ranchers, farmers, shop-keepers, gamblers, and some others of disrepute. The numbers swelled as word spread. Seventy-five, one hundred, two hundred, three hundred. Near every man in the county answered the call. Men reported to the sheriff's office awaiting the time.

"Hell of a show of force, Sheriff," Dan Shaw said.

Whitaker nodded.

"How will we know when to ride?"

Whitaker smiled. "When you tell us, Dan."

"Me? How will I know?"

"You're going to ride down N bar C and keep an eye on the place. When the bad guys show up, you come fetch us. Can you do that?"

"I'll head down there in the morning."

"Good."

Johnson County Line

Ruben Toller saw dust sign. Plenty of it headed north. He reined his horse west on a line to cross their trail. He drew rein to watch the cloud grow. Riders resolved out from under it. *Sure, as the world, comin' in force. Hope this works.*

McGant saw him first. Lone rider, watching and waiting. He called a halt at hailing distance.

"Who are you and what do you want?"

"Name's not important. What you come for is. You'll find 'em at N Bar C Ranch northwest of here."

"Why you tellin' us this?"

"Got a score to settle. Figure you'll do it for me."

"If that ranch has the start of what we came for, count on it."

"How'd you know we was comin'?"

"Didn't. Saw your dust sign. Just lucky I guess."

Toller wheeled his horse and squeezed up a lope east.

Chesterfield eased his horse up beside

McGant. "What do you make of it, Buck?"

"I know the N Bar C Ranch. Neighbors my MC spread. Nate Champion's one of 'em. His place is as good a place to start as any."

"Still that jasper happening on us like he did is a lot to credit to chance. What if they know we're comin'?"

"How would they know?"

Davis shrugged.

"Even if they do, what difference does it make? We got fifty of the best guns in the territory backin' our play. We'll give the place the once over before we take it down."

McGant led out northwest.

N Bar C Ranch

From a stand of white oak on a hilltop southeast of N Bar C Ranch, Dan Shaw spotted dust-sign big enough it could only mean one thing. He swung up on his horse and lit out for Buffalo.

Cane kept lookout from the barn loft.

"Here they come!"

Longstreet and Champion took up their positions.

The invaders drew a halt. They fanned out along a broad front. A big man broke ranks and rode in. Cane recognized Buck McGant.

"Yo the house!"

"What do you want?"

"You out. You got two hours to clear out before we burn you out."

"Go to hell."

"Suit yourself. Give you a taste of where you're headed." McGant rejoined his men.

A dozen riders advanced on the left, another on the right.

"They're fixin' to surround us," Cane called.

Longstreet laid down a warning shot ahead of the lead on the left. Cane did the same on the right. A volley of return fire erupted along the line in the center. Longstreet fired twice taking down the lead rider on the left and the next man up. That sent the invaders leaping from their horses and diving for cover. Cane picked off the lead rider on the right and marked cover positions taken by the haze of powder smoke rising over each. He smiled. *Looky there. Right where we want 'em.*

"Hold your fire!" McGant's command echoed along his line. The shooting went quiet. "You want to play this the hard way, Champion. Fine. Your choice. It'll be dark in a few hours. Then we burn you out."

Time enough for Whitaker's posse to get here. Longstreet smiled.

Cane checked his arrows and fuses. He crossed to the right side of the loft door where he had a view north. *When the sheriff and his posse arrive, we'll give the invaders a proper welcome surprise.*

Two hours later Whitaker and his men appeared in the distance on the trail from town. Cane slipped back to the left side of the loft door. He lit a cheroot selecting the arrow and fuse for his easiest shot. He checked his trajectory note and nocked the arrow. Touching the fuse to light, he drew, set his aim, and let fly. The arrow flew a graceful arc. No one saw it coming until the charge detonated just before striking the ground. A gout of dirt and rock obliterated the nearby cover position. Two bodies were thrown in the air. Others scrambled away. Cane selected his next arrow.

"What the hell was that?" McGant's ears rang deaf on his own question.

"Dynamite!" Someone screamed.

"Here comes another one!"

The invaders broke, fighting to catch frightened mounts. The second explosion erupted in chaotic melee.

"Look there!"

McGant followed the man's point to a force of several hundred riding down on them.

"Let's get out of here! Now!"

"Where to?"

"My MC Ranch. We can hole up there."

As they mounted up, McGant grabbed Chesterfield's horse by the bridle. "Davis, circle back to Buffalo. We're gonna need the governor's help. Tell him to call out the army, there's an insurrection in Johnson County!"

Chesterfield peeled away west. McGant led his invaders southeast.

CHAPTER TWENTY-SEVEN

O'Rourke House
Denver
1911

I arrived the following Saturday with my
stain selection and brushes wrapped in
brown paper. I agonized over the decision. I
would have felt better about it if Penny
made it for me, but as this was to be a
surprise, I found myself left to my own
devices. Walnut or golden oak, how to
decide. The walnut did indeed have a rich-
ness to it as Angela suggested, though I
feared for the loss of the grain. Golden oak,
the hardware man informed me, was a stain
to enhance the appearance of grain in the
wood. What to do? What would Penny like?
Who could know such a thing, given the
pattern of our wedding choices? This much
I knew, she didn't prefer the style of the set
we were given. What if I should further
bungle it by the wrong choice of a stain?

Mired in misgiving, I was, am, and remain.

Angela answered my knock.

"Robert, dear, what have we here? Have you made a stain selection?"

"I have." The moment of truth. Could one woman reveal the preference of another?

"And how did you choose?"

"With great difficulty. The walnut truly has an elegant look."

"As I told you it would."

"Then there is the beautiful grain in the wood. I couldn't bear the thought of covering it up. So, I've chosen the golden oak."

"I see."

She doesn't like it.

"Good choice, lad," Briscoe said halfway down the stairs. "It's right for the wood as even Angela will see once we've completed our work. Shall we adjourn to the carriage house and prove our point?"

And we did. Adjourn to the carriage house. Point proving would remain to be seen. Not a result available in abundance when it comes to taste in men and a woman's preference in my limited experience.

N Bar C Ranch

Sheriff Whitaker rode in at the head of a militia-strength posse.

"Don't look like you needed us to break

up the party. That was some fireworks display."

"Briscoe's right handy with dynamite when called for," Longstreet said.

Cane came out of the barn, Henry and bow in hand, saddlebags over his shoulder.

Champion shook his head in amazement. "Glad I got to see that, even if you made a couple of holes in my ranch."

"Better holes than burnt out."

"Sheriff, I'm guessin' the party ain't over that easy," Longstreet said. "Any idea where they're headed?"

"There's a Wyoming Stock Growers Association member ranch southeast of here. Looks like that might be where they're headed."

"Then I think we best get after them. Return the favor until they decide to clear out of Johnson County."

"We'll get to it."

"We'll get our horses and catch up."

"Nate here can show you the way."

MC Ranch
McGant and his invaders forted up in the ranch house, barn, bunkhouse, and toolshed. The ranch headquarters bristled with gun barrels.

Sheriff Whitaker and his posse had the

invaders surrounded when Longstreet, Cane, and Champion rode in. They found Whitaker and stepped down.

"How you figure on playing this, Sheriff?" Longstreet said.

"They gotta eat."

"You're sayin' wait 'em out?"

"You got a better suggestion?"

"Briscoe could give 'em a dose of dynamite."

"That'd smoke 'em out sure. Also get us a firefight. I got a lot of good people out here. Neighbors and friends, I don't want to see anybody get hurt."

"Alright then. We play it your way."

The standoff settled into a siege of attrition. Time passed to the next day.

Maddie. Must be worried sick. "Briscoe."

"Yeah."

"With nothing going on here, I'm going to take a ride into town."

"What's on your mind?"

"Maddie."

"Alright my friend. We'll hold the fort here."

"I'll be back directly."

Beau swung into his saddle and headed for town.

Western Union Office
Buffalo

Davis Chesterfield scratched out his note on the counter. He handed it to the telegrapher and listened as it rattled down the line to Cheyenne.

Governor Amos Barber
Insurrection in Johnson County stop.
Ranchers and stock detectives under siege at MC Ranch stop.
Urgent need for military to put down revolt and restore order stop.
Davis

Cheyenne
Governor's Office

"Telegram, Governor."

Barber tore open the envelop and read. *Insurrection. Siege. Urgent need for military aid. Military.* Hell, this is the territorial governor's office. Military needs presidential orders. Davis and Buck have bought themselves a passel of trouble this time. Who knows if I draw enough water in Washington to pull this off? Only one way to find out. He scratched Davis's plea to a sheet of official stationery.

"Thomas!"

"Sir?"

262

"Need you to run this to Western Union now."

Thomas looked at the message eyes wide. "Yes, sir." He turned on his heel and headed for the door. Minutes later Governor Barber's request rattled down the line to a date with destiny in Washington, D.C.

President Chester A. Arthur
Insurrection in Johnson County Wyoming Territory stop.
Ranchers and stock detectives under siege at MC Ranch stop.
Urgent need for military to put down rebellion and restore order stop.
Amos Barber, Governor

White House
Washington, DC

President Arthur shook his head, scratched a bushy sideburn, and read the telegram a second time. Never heard of Johnson County, wherever the hell that is. Insurrection? Strong word to be throwing around. What might provoke an insurrection against ranchers and stock detectives? There had to be more to this. Calling out the military in a civilian matter came highly regulated by the Posse Comitatus Act President Hayes signed in '78. You didn't do it at the drop of

263

a hat. Still you had the territorial governor alarmed enough to call for the army to intervene. What to do?

Arthur rose from his desk, clasped his hand behind his back, and paced to the window for a view of the gardens. Something about nature cleansed the spirit for critical thinking. Without knowledge of the situation on the ground provoking the call for help, he had little to go on. The governor called it insurrection. Insurrection lent gravity to the situation. He shouldn't question the judgment from this office. Better to rely on a disciplined set of eyes at the scene.

"Wellington."

"Mr. President," the assistant appeared at the office door.

"Take a telegram, please."

Fort McKinney
Wyoming Territory
Colonel Josiah Cobb stood ramrod straight on a windswept parade ground prepared to conduct his weekly inspection. The regiment, men and mounts, drawn up before him in orderly ranks. Spit and polish from brass to boots and tack were the order of the day. Cobb ran a tight ship, to borrow a term from his father's naval career. Cobb opted for West Point, having not inherited

his father's "sea legs." An expression he preferred to an admission of sea sickness.

A corporal appeared at his elbow as he was about to step off on inspecting the ranks.

"Telegram, sir."

"Can it keep, Corporal? I'm busy here."

"It's from the White House, sir."

Cobb paused mid-stride. He tore open the envelop.

Commanding Officer
Fort McKinney
Governor Barber requests aid to put down reported insurrection stop.
This order is subject to lawful provisions of Posse Comitatus Act stop.
You are to proceed to MC Ranch, Johnson County stop.
Use means and measures necessary to restore order stop.
Chester A. Arthur, President.

"Sergeant Major."

"Sir."

"Dismiss the regiment. A, C, and D companies. Boots and Saddles. We ride within the hour."

"Yes, sir."

Longstreet wheeled Yankee to the front gate. He dropped from the saddle, looping a rein over the fence. He swung through the gate and strode up the walk. He rapped on the door. The door flung open to misty green eyes. She melted into his arms.

"I'm so glad you're here. I've been worried sick. The town is buzzing with rumor."

He held her tight. "I thought you might be worried. I decided to let you know I'm alright."

"I'm so happy you did." She tipped up her toes to his lips. The moment dissolved. Breathless. "Come in." She led the way to the parlor settee. "Tell me all of it."

"Not much to tell. McGant and his invaders took the bait at N Bar C Ranch. Briscoe made a little dynamite rain. Sheriff Whitaker and the biggest posse the territory's ever seen showed up right on time. The invaders tucked tail between their legs and ran. They've forted up at MC Ranch. We've got the place surrounded. Figure to starve 'em out."

"No shooting?"

"Not since we ran 'em off N bar C."

"And you took the time to let me know you're alright. Might make a girl think the man cares."

"That girl better know. Seems like I told her I love her."

"You did. She just likes to hear it."

"Good."

She rested her head on his chest, snug in the crook of his arm for a time.

"What's to become of us when this is over?"

"I'm workin' on that."

"Working on what?"

"What's possible. A bridge we can cross when we come to it."

"There's a bridge?"

"There is. We just have to find it."

"I like the sound of that too. When do you have to head back?"

"In the morning, if you can spare me this settee until then."

"You have changed."

"Told you."

"I'm glad, I think."

"Now don't go wobbly on my newfound gentle-manhood."

"You're the boss."

"You've changed too."

"Grown some."

"Me too."

CHAPTER TWENTY-EIGHT

MC Ranch

Longstreet rode in midmorning under a blazing hot sun. Cane greeted him as he stepped down.

"Welcome back."

"Any developments here?"

"More of the same. It's like McGant thinks something is going to get him out of this. How's Maddie? You two pickin' up where you left off?"

"That'd be nice. I just don't yet know what's possible."

"Hope it works out for both of you."

"Nothing's gonna happen until this is over. Where's Sheriff Whitaker?"

Cane lifted his chin, pointing him out down the line.

"Come on." Longstreet led the way along the line to the sheriff.

"Sheriff Whitaker."

"Longstreet."

"How long you plan to wait these boys out?"

"Starvation takes a while."

"What happens if the press of daily life forces some of your posse to go home?"

"A few have left."

"More will."

"You have a better idea?"

"Squeeze 'em."

"How?"

"Build a siege wagon."

"A what?"

"Siege wagon, kinda like a Trojan horse."

"Horses pull wagons."

Longstreet chuckled. "Not a siege wagon. We take a wagon and build a barricade a few men can take cover behind. Then we back it up close enough Briscoe can wave a little dynamite under their nose. They either come out with hands up or . . ."

"That might oughta get 'em out at that."

"It might. Let's find us a wagon."

Champion had a wagon and the makings for a barricade driven over from his ranch. They built it into a siege wagon in a few hours and in plain sight of ranch headquarters. They positioned the barricade at the back of the wagon. This allowed the wagon to be backed forward with the men behind it in control of steering and the brake.

Longstreet and Cane took up positions behind the barricade as the wagon started forward. As the wagon closed on the barn it was greeted by a volley of gunfire. Longstreet set the brake.

"McGant!"

"What?"

"You remember the fireworks display back at N bar C?"

No answer.

"You got a choice. Throw down your guns and come out, or we bring this ranch down around your ears."

Silence.

"Well, McGant, what's it gonna be?"

Silence.

"Looks like he might need a little encouragement."

Cane peeked around the barricade. "Got a real nice porch across the front of that ranch house. Be a shame to knock down this end."

"Actions have consequences. So do inactions."

"Thought you might see it that way."

Cane drew a glow on the tip of his cheroot. The fuse sparked a hiss. He watched it a moment, then threw. The stick arced toward the house. Warning shouts and bodies scrambled within as the stick bounced on the porch, exploding in a bloom of smoke, splinters, and a shower of shingles.

"Hold your fire. We're coming out."

"Throw out your guns first. Then come out of the house with your hands where we can see 'em. Bunkhouse is next. Barn after that." Longstreet signaled the sheriff to move in.

McGant and the men in the house threw out their guns and stepped into sunlight, blinking.

"Bunkhouse, you're next."

More guns pitched into the yard. Sullen men followed, hands in the air.

"Now the barn."

With forty-odd men accounted for, deputies covered the prisoners while others gathered their guns.

"Gotta hand it to you, Longstreet," Whitaker said. "That went slick as snot off a bull's nose."

At that a bugle call rang through the air. A long blue column, three-companies strong, rode in from the northwest and drew a halt.

"Who's in charge here?"

"That'd be me, Johnson County Sheriff, Ben Whitaker. And you?"

"Colonel Josiah Cobb, commanding officer Fort McKinney." Cobb dismounted.

"What brings you here, Colonel?"

"We are here by order of President Arthur. Governor Barber requested military assistance in putting down an insurrection in Johnson County."

"Ain't no insurrection in Johnson County, other than bein' invaded by these Wyoming stock growers' hired guns. They're all under arrest and in my custody."

A civilian riding with the cavalry rode forward. "Colonel, there ain't no law in Johnson County. Only rebels in a state of armed insurrection. These men were sent here to clean out a rat's nest of rustlers."

"And who might you be?" Whitaker asked.

"Davis Chesterfield. I'm the one alerted Governor Barber."

"Now, Colonel, if you'll excuse us, we need to take our prisoners into town."

"Colonel, these me were sent here with the full knowledge of the governor to deal with rampant lawlessness. Lawlessness that has deteriorated into a state of open revolt."

"I'm afraid I can't allow that, Sheriff. You and your men are to disburse this unlawful assembly and go to your homes. My orders are to restore order."

"Unlawful assembly? I'm the duly elected sheriff of Johnson County. These men are my deputies. These others are my prisoners in a civil matter."

"I'm afraid this is no longer a civil matter in a county declared to be in a state of civil unrest on the authority of the territorial governor. I am taking custody of these men and will turn them over to the governor. Now I'll say it once more. You and your men are to disburse and go to your homes. Should you fail to obey my order, I am authorized to use force to restore order."

Whitaker looked to Longstreet. Beau shook his head.

"Mount up, boys, but hang on to them guns."

Cobb watched the posse head back to town. "Captain Barnette."

"Sir."

"A company will escort these men to Casper and accompany them to Cheyenne by train. There you will turn them over to Governor Barber with my compliments. If the governor is satisfied the situation is resolved, wire his response to Fort McKinney."

"Yes, sir." Barnette gave a crisp salute. "A Company, guard detail front and center!"

CHAPTER TWENTY-NINE

15 Aspen Lane
Denver
1911

The day finally arrived. With finishing touches on the kitchen set complete under Briscoe's watchful eye, we loaded it on a rented wagon and drove it to our new home, empty now save the settee, Mrs. David having moved back east. We next drove the wagon to our apartment where we dismantled and loaded our bed. We loaded our personal effects, completing the move to our new home. Briscoe helped us unload and reassemble the bed before departing to return the wagon.

We looked around our virtually empty new home. We hugged and kissed, sensing the opening of an important new chapter in our marriage.

"I have something to show you."

"A surprise?"

"A surprise."

"I love it."

"How do you know?"

"What's not to love about a surprise?"

"Let's see."

The moment of truth arrived as we walked into the kitchen. There stood a golden oak new old kitchen set. She clapped her hands.

"Robert! It's beautiful. Where did you get it? How could we afford it?"

"Angela had it stored in her carriage house. Briscoe taught me how to refinish it."

"You did this?"

"I did."

"I love it!"

"The last time you saw a set like this you said didn't 'prefer' Mrs. David's set."

"Mrs. David's set didn't have your touch to it. This is so special."

We kissed again. And again.

"Help me move it," Penny said.

"Move it? Where?"

"To the dining room. It's too pretty to leave in the kitchen and it will give that room a feeling of finish."

All my anxiety endured for naught. We moved the newly christened dining room set to its proper place. At which point we kissed some more.

"Let's be sure," Penny purred.

"Be sure of what?"

She took me by the hand and led me upstairs.

"Be sure the bed is properly put together."

We did. It was.

O'Rourke House
1911

Briscoe answered my knock a week later with Angela answering from the kitchen.

"How did Penny like the kitchen set?" they asked almost in unison.

"She loved it. In fact, it has been promoted."

"Promoted?" Briscoe lifted a questioning brow.

"To the dining room," Angela clapped with a dazzling smile.

"Why yes. How did you know?"

"She loved it because you did the work."

"Well yes, but how did you know that?"

"What woman wouldn't?"

Briscoe and I exchanged mystified glances.

"Even if it wasn't walnut?" I couldn't resist.

"Even if it wasn't walnut, though walnut surely would have added a touch of elegance to the dining room."

I should have resisted.

"Come along, Robert. Where were we?"

Shaw Ranch

Buffalo Bulletin

Sheriff Whitaker routes Wyoming Stock Growers Association Invaders Backed by Citizen Posse

A force of some fifty professional gunmen in the employ of the Wyoming Stock Growers Association invaded Johnson County this past week, mounting an assault on Nate Champion's N Bar C Ranch in southwestern Johnson County. Sheriff Whitaker, and a citizen posse numbering near three hundred deputies, repulsed the assault and pursued the invaders who took shelter at MC Ranch owned by WSGA President Buck McGant. A siege ensued. The standoff ended when cavalry out of Fort McKinney took charge of Sheriff Whitaker's prisoners by order of President Chester A. Arthur, following a formal request for assistance by Wyoming Governor Amos Barber.

Sheriff Whitaker has served the people of Johnson County with distinction for more than a decade never more valiantly than in the face of the hostilities reported here. In a related announcement Sheriff Whitaker tells the *Bulletin* he plans to retire at the end of his current term.

Dan handed Longstreet the paper and watched as he read. Longstreet handed the paper back.

"Sheriff Whitaker is a good man. Big boots to fill."

"You need to fill 'em, Beau."

"Me? I don't even live in Johnson County. It's an elected position. No one knows who I am."

"Wrong. Every man in that posse knows who you are and what you done. As for not living in Johnson County, I can think of at least one citizen who might be pleased to hear you take up residence."

"Can I have the paper?"

"Be my guest."

Sheriff's Office
Buffalo, Wyoming Territory

Longstreet reined Yankee in at the rail and stepped down. Late afternoon sun slanted between long building shadows up and down High Street buffeted by gusts of Wyoming's warmest hospitality. He found Sheriff Whitaker at his desk.

278

"Longstreet, glad you're here. You was on my list to look up."

"Why would that be?"

"Maybe you haven't heard the news. I'm plannin' to retire at the end of my term."

"I did hear that. Thought I'd drop by to offer my best wishes."

"I'd like to bend your ear on something more than that. Have a seat."

Beau did. "What's on your mind?"

"After seein' all you done for the Shaws and the way you handled the stock growers' invasion, strikes me you'd be just the feller to take this job after me."

"I'm honored you think so."

"Johnson County needs a good man. I'd feel better about leavin' if I was to know I left the folks in capable hands."

"It's an elected position, Ben. I don't even live in the county."

"The election ain't until November. If I was to take you on as a deputy, people would get to know you. I s'pect my endorsement is worth a little somethin'. Besides every man on that posse knows what you done."

"Dan Shaw said the same. He put me up to comin' to see you. He thinks I should run too."

"What do you think?"

"Not sure I know just yet. If your offer of a deputy job is on the table, I'll figure it out in a day or so."

"Fair enough." Whitaker stood to shake Longstreet's hand.

Hart Street

Purple shadow crawled out the western mountains as Longstreet tied up at Maddie's gate. He drew a bottle of good Irish whiskey from his saddlebag, opened the gate to a now familiar chirp, and started up an eventful walk. He tapped on the door. It swung open to the moment.

"Hi, handsome. What have you got there?"

"Noticed you were a little low last time."

"No thanks to you." She smiled. "Come on in. I'll pour us a finger."

"Make it two." Longstreet hung his hat on the coat-tree and found his way to the parlor settee. Maddie came to him, glasses in hand.

"So, I guess this is it," she said with a wistful look in her eye.

"This is what?"

"Trouble's over. You'll be headed back to Denver."

"Is that what you want?"

Moments passed.

"No."

"What if I was to find reason to stay?"

"You mean give up the league?"

"If I was to stay."

"I'll not ask that of you."

"You did that once. Did it change anything? Did it change the way you feel about me?"

"No. You know that."

"Did it change the way I feel about you?"

She lifted a tearful eye.

"Remember, as I recall we were seated on the settee in the O'Rourke House parlor with a couple glasses of this." He held up his glass.

"There's more you know."

She knit her brow and tilted her chin in her inquisitive way.

He took her glass and set them both on the side table.

"You're loved."

Her eyes glistened moist.

He kissed her, gently.

"Beau Longstreet, did I just hear what I think I heard?"

"If you heard me say 'I love you,' you did."

She traced the line of his jaw with a finger.

"There's more than that."

More? The word invaded her gaze.

"If you'll have me, Maddie O'Rourke, will you marry me?"

"Oh, Beau." A tear welled in one eye.

"Tears? Is it that bad?"

"No, love. It's so . . . so much all at once."

"You can't think it sudden. We've been traveling this path for some time now."

"We have and I felt it too. It's only . . ."

"It's only we lost each other to hesitation. It didn't change our feelings for one another. I don't want to let that happen ever again."

"Oh, Beau." Her head came to rest on his chest

He held her close. "Now listen. Sheriff Whitaker is retiring."

"I did hear something about that."

"Ben wants me to run for sheriff. He's offered me a deputy's job until the election. Kind of make me his choice. He says after what I did against the invaders every man on that posse will back me. Is that something you could live with?"

"If that will keep you here with me . . . yes, Beau Longstreet, yes!"

"Then, Maddie O'Rourke, for the last time . . ." He slipped off the settee to a knee. "Will you marry me?"

She took his face in her hands, beaming on tear streaked checks. "Yes, Beau Longstreet, yes!"

He took her in his arms and kissed her tears away. "Seems like you cried the last time I asked you that."

"Silly girl."

"I like the taste of these tears better."

Time lapsed, warm and tender, sweet. Hearts twined, surrendered in love.

CHAPTER THIRTY

Cheyenne

Deputy Seth Adams watched them detrain. The stock growers' mighty invasion force came home under military escort, disarmed, disheveled, and defeated. McGant and Chesterfield were going to clean up Johnson county. Wonder what happened? He smiled to himself. Likely Beau Longstreet had a hand in it.

Cheyenne Daily Leader

**Lawlessness Continues
in Johnson County
Wyoming Stock Growers Association
Stock Detectives Assaulted**

Wyoming Stock Growers stock detectives were attacked by rogue elements in Johnson County while investigating allegations of cattle rustling by Nate Champion, owner of the N Bar C Ranch. A large force of armed gunmen forced the detectives to take shelter at Buck McGant's MC Ranch northern headquarters where they were surrounded and threatened with dynamite. Fortunately, Governor Amos Barber was alerted to the threat. Governor Barber petitioned President Arthur in Washington to call out the army to put down the insurrection. Soldiers from Fort McKinney lifted the MC Ranch siege, disbursed the vigilantes, and escorted the stock detectives to safety.

Seth folded the paper. Stock detectives investigating a rustling accusation. You need fifty gunmen to do that investigation? No doubt the opposition was anything but lawless vigilantes.

Sheriff's Office
Buffalo
Cane tied Smoke at the rail, freshened by a late summer breeze, whispering a hint of things about to change. He stepped up the boardwalk and entered the office. He found Deputy Longstreet with Sheriff Whitaker.

"Sheriff, Beau. You seen this?" He laid the paper on the desk, for both of them to read.

Buffalo Bulletin

Governor Barber Orders Johnson County Invaders Released

Justice for Johnson County comes up short in the governor's office. Governor Amos Barber orders release of all those implicated in the recent attack on Nate Champion's N Bar C Ranch. What comes next? Where do the citizens of Johnson County turn for justice? Cattle barons may own the governor's office. They don't own Johnson County. Clearly it will be up to us to defend ourselves.

"What do you make of it, Beau?" Whitaker asked.

"McGant won't give it up."

"Likely not. We'll have to keep our eyes peeled."

"Well, I guess this is it." Cane said.

"You headin' out?"

"I am. Anything you want me to tell the Colonel?"

"I wired him I'd be staying here in Buffalo. Tell him how much I appreciate all he and the league have done for me these past years. Tell him he can add Buffalo to league's network."

"I will. Things won't be the same without

you, Longstreet. We've done some good work together."

"We have. One last thing."

"Sure."

"When you get to Cheyenne, look up Deputy Seth Adams. I worked with him on the bank fraud case. Real promise there. He'd be a good man if the Colonel is looking to replace me."

"Seth Adams. Will do. Take care of yourself, pard. And Maddie too."

"Count on it. You take care too." They shook hands.

"I expect our trails will cross again."

"Likely so. 'Til then."

"Sheriff."

"Thanks for all your help, Briscoe. You and your fireworks are welcome in Buffalo anytime."

"Much obliged."

Cattlemen's Club
Cheyenne

"Damned laughingstock is what the son of a bitch made of us." McGant stormed as he paced the high-stakes game room. "I'll not stand for it."

"Somebody tipped them off," Chesterfield said.

"Had to, but who?"

287

"Somebody here or up in Casper."

"All those preparations took time. Likely the warning came from here."

"Sheriff Tyler, I'd wager."

"Likely so. We need to make an example. Send a message."

"Sheriff Tyler?"

"No. Too close to home. We make an example of the tin star in Buffalo."

"Whitaker?"

"Yeah. He's the one made us look like fools. This time, they won't see us comin'."

"Who's going?"

"Me and Cole Hardy."

"Good choice. When?"

"Soon."

Ace High Saloon
Cheyenne

McGant found Hardy working on a bottle of whiskey in the company of two other gunslicks.

"Cole, can I buy you a drink?"

"Got one."

"To talk business."

"That's different." He scraped his chair back and followed McGant to a back-corner table.

McGant signaled the bartender. Whiskies arrived directly.

"What's on your mind?"

"Tin star in Johnson County made fools of us. I plan to make an example of him."

"I believe I'd enjoy that. You know my terms."

"Your fee will be paid once the body is cold."

"When we leave?"

"Morning train to Casper. Meet me at the depot. I'll have your ticket for you. You'll need your horse for the ride up to Buffalo."

Sheriff's Office
Cheyenne

Cane found young Adams in the office leafing through a stack of wanted dodgers.

"Mr. Cane, welcome back to Cheyenne. Sheriff's out if you're lookin' for him."

"Actually, I came to see you."

"Me? What can I do for you?"

"Beau Longstreet thought we should talk. He was impressed by the way you handled yourself on the bank fraud case."

"Nice to hear. Where is Mr. Longstreet?"

"He's staying in Buffalo. He found what he came for. That's why he thought we should talk. Beau leaving the league means we have room for another officer. Be a step up for a competent young man such as yourself."

"Guess we better talk then."

"I'm staying at Rawlins House. Can you meet me there at six for some supper?"

"Best offer I had all day. I'm guessing you and Mr. Longstreet had a hand in that dustup in Johnson County. I'd be interested to hear your side of it. All we got here is the cattle growers' side of a newspaper story."

"Fair enough. See you at six."

CHAPTER THIRTY-ONE

Rawlins House

Cane and Adams took a quiet table across the room from the only two other diners. They ordered steaks.

"So, tell me about the Great Western Detective League."

"It's an association of law enforcement professionals across the west. It was founded by Colonel David Crook who runs it out of offices in Denver. Members cooperate in investigating crimes and criminals that cross local jurisdictions."

"Like when Mr. Longstreet notified the sheriffs along the U.P. line to be on the lookout for the bank fraudsters."

"That's right. In that case Beau had a pretty good idea where the men he wanted were headed. In another circumstance, if he needed a broader lookout, he'd notify the Colonel in Denver who'd send out a general alert to all the league offices or all those that fit the circumstances of the case."

"And everyone cooperates because the money is good."

Cane smiled. "That's right. How'd you know?"

"Beau was kind enough to cut me in on the reward for recovering the bank funds."

"Most of the cases the league handles come with rewards or recoveries offered. I hunted bounty before joining the league. I was from Missouri when the Colonel approached me about joining up. He talked me into giving it a try on the Sam Bass case. Me and my poke have never looked back. Would that interest you?"

"Sure. What do I have to do?"

"If you were to take Beau's place, you'd have to move to Denver."

Seth shrugged. "Nothing holding me here."

"I can't promise you that position. That will be up to the Colonel, but Beau has spoken highly of you to him already. I'm headed back to Denver tomorrow. Why not come with me and meet Colonel Crook?"

"I got a little time off coming, give me a day to let Sheriff Tyler know I'll be taking a couple days off."

"I can do that."

"Now tell me, what happened when the

stock growers invaded Johnson County?"

"Thanks to your wire to Beau, we were ready for 'em. We set an ambush for them at N Bar C Ranch. Roughed 'em up a bit before Sheriff Whitaker run 'em off with a little posse of about three hundred."

"Three hundred?"

"Like I said, we were ready for 'em. They lit out for McGant's MC Ranch and holed up. We surrounded 'em. Threatened 'em with a little more rough stuff and they decided to give up."

"You keep sayin' 'rough.' What's rough?"

"Dynamite."

"That's rough. How'd the army get involved?"

"Good question. Somehow, they got word they were in trouble to Governor Barber. I suspect it was that Davis Chesterfield fella who rode with the cavalry."

"Chesterfield is an officer with the stock growers' association."

"Barber managed to convince President Arthur no less to call out the army. Pretty rare for that to happen in a civil matter."

"Cattle barons draw a lot of water with the powers that be. Governor Barber likely owes his office to those boys. Too bad in this case. That put the governor in charge, and he let 'em all off."

"Politics. It happens."

Cheyenne Station

As part of his regular rounds Seth made a habit of checking the depot when trains arrived and departed. Next morning under a bright and cloudless sky, he watched as Buck McGant and hired gun Cole Hardy loaded horses on the train to Casper. Seth smelled trouble. *Horses said they'd be movin' on from Casper.* Another tip to Beau Longstreet couldn't hurt.

Sheriff's Office
Buffalo

> *Cheyenne*
> *Be on lookout stop.*
> *Buck McGant and Cole Hardy believed headed your way stop.*
> *Seth*

Longstreet handed the telegram to Sheriff Whitaker.

"Who's Cole Hardy?" Whitaker asked.

"Gunslick. Trouble for hire."

"What do you suppose McGant is up to?"

"No good, though that don't narrow it down none. Revenge if I had to guess."

"That don't narrow it down none neither."

"Might."

"Then who?"

"You."

"Me?"

"You made McGant look pretty stupid. Man with a self-opinion big as his, might take personal offense to that."

"I s'pose."

"Best we keep a sharp eye out."

"Best."

Hart Street

Longstreet took a room in town to establish a Johnson County address. Given their history, Maddie took a personal interest in approving the accommodation. After that, Beau's duties permitting, supper on Hart Street became a regular thing, followed by tender time on the porch swing, swathed in starlight.

"What sort of wedding do you want?"

She had that look in her eye he liked. "One that makes you my wife."

"Well that is a good start, but where, a church, the courthouse?"

"What do you want?"

"A small church wedding feels right."

"Then a small church wedding it shall be. Have a church in mind?"

295

"I've been to services at First Methodist on Adams Street. Pastor Austin is a very nice man. You should meet him sometime."

"Sometime soon."

She smiled. He kissed her.

"Soon." She sighed. "Do you miss it?"

"Miss it?"

"You know, Denver, the league?"

"I'll miss Briscoe and the Colonel, for all his irascible ways, but nothing compared to the way I missed you. I feel whole again for the first time since before the war."

"I'm glad. I feel whole again for the first time in . . . a very long time. For too long I was afraid to trust myself with the possibility I might love again. Then you came along and made a mockery of my fortress."

"Look where it got you."

"Happy and in love."

"See. Actually, I rather enjoyed the mockery."

"I'm sure you did."

"Remember . . ."

"Who's there?"

"It's Beau."

She appeared in the dining room, wiping her hands on her apron. An errant tendril of auburn hair hung loose from the pile of curls on top of her head. Flour smeared one cheek. She looked lovely.

"Well look what the cat dragged in."

"I suppose I am a bit shabby after three days on the stage from Santa Fe."

She crossed the dining room to the foyer. "Is Samantha home as well?"

"She'll be along directly. I suspect she's making her report to Kingsley."

"And did you two have a successful trip?"

"After a fashion. We captured two of the counterfeiters we were after and the bogus bonds they were passing. The ringleaders escaped."

"Well at least you had the pleasure of keeping company."

"Miss Maples is a colleague and a competitor at that. There was no company keeping involved."

"Of course not, and none of my concern if there were."

"You brought it up."

"My mistake. Welcome home to you. I'm sure you'll want to freshen up. Supper is at six-thirty."

"Did you miss me?"

"Did I miss you? I've no intention to flatter you, Beau Longstreet. You flatter yourself more than enough for all of us."

"But did you miss me?"

"You're impossible!"

"Lovable too."

"Ugh!" She reddened, turned on her heel, and stomped back to the kitchen.

"You missed me."

"Didn't want to."

"And now?"

"I know."

"Promise me you won't forget."

"I won't."

"Here's to mockery." His kiss reached the edge of her soul.

"I'll make us an appointment to meet Reverend Austin . . . soon."

"Very soon."

CHAPTER THIRTY-TWO

*Great Western Detective League Offices
Denver*

Colonel Crook sat at his desk, haloed in bright morning sun, streaming through the windows behind him. Desktop neat save a stack of overnight communiques from various league offices, a fresh cup of coffee steamed at his elbow. Cane appeared at the door, accompanied by a solidly built young man.

"Colonel?"

"Briscoe, welcome back. And who might this be?" He rose.

"Colonel Crook meet Seth Adams. You may remember Beau mentioned him when he returned from Cheyenne."

"I do recall. Pleased to meet you, Seth. Beau spoke highly of your work on the bank fraud case. Come in. Have a seat. What brings you to Denver?"

"Briscoe's been telling me about the

league. He thought I should see you about the possibility of replacing Mr. Longstreet."

"I see."

"I'll leave you two to get acquainted," Cane said taking his leave.

"Have a seat, Seth. Tell me about yourself."

"Not much to tell. Grew up on a small ranch in Kansas. My parents passed away a few years ago. Ranching wasn't in my blood. My brothers took over the place. I pulled up stakes and headed west. Hit Cheyenne on the heels of a stage robbery. Sheriff Tyler was raising a posse. I needed work so I signed on. Helped bring the outlaws in and recover the gold shipment they stole. Sheriff Tyler offered me a deputy's job. I needed work. Took the job. Been with him three years now."

"Beau tells me you have a knack for investigative work. Why do you think that is?"

"Common sense. I figure things out. Been trackin' since I was old enough to tote a gun and hunt. That's likely some of it."

Crook smiled. "Makes sense. You interested in joining the league?"

"That's why I'm here."

"Willing to come to Denver and work out of this office?"

"Nothing holding me to Cheyenne."

"How soon could you start?"

"Owe Sheriff Tyler a little time to find a replacement. Say first of the month, unless Habb finds someone sooner."

"Fair enough." Crook rose and offered his hand. "Welcome to the Great Western Detective League."

Cane approached Seth as he left the Colonel's office.

"Well?"

"Looks like I'll be coming to Denver next month."

"Good. Meantime I'll see if Beau's landlady still has his room. I think she might. You might as well have it."

"Much obliged. One less thing to think on."

The office door swung open. Seth clenched his jaw to keep it from dropping open.

"Samantha," Cane said. "What brings you here?"

"Which here? Denver? Transfer. This office? Longstreet, he around?"

"Beau's now deputy sheriff in Johnson County."

She smiled. "Not surprised. He headed north like a love-sick pup the moment the right finger crooked."

"So, you've been transferred to Denver."

"Have. Reggie finally convinced Chicago there was enough work here to keep me engaged." She paused, noticing Seth with an appraising violet eye. "Well, well, what have we here?"

"Seth Adams, meet notorious Pinkerton Agent, Samantha Maples."

"Notorious? You flatter me, Briscoe. Never knew you noticed."

"I'm an investigator too remember."

"Pinkerton?" Seth found his voice.

"Disarming, isn't it," Samantha said.

"Sorry Miss Maples. I meant no offense."

"None taken. And Miss Maples goes by Samantha."

"Seth is joining the league to take Beau's place. Moving here next month from Cheyenne."

"I see. So, you'll be new in town too?"

"Yes, ma'am."

"Yes, Sam."

"Yes, Sam."

"That's better. The league and Pinkerton sometimes wind up working on the same cases. We should have a drink sometime and get acquainted."

"I, I'd like that. Maybe when I get back from Cheyenne."

"When are you leaving?"

"Tomorrow."

"Mmm . . . you staying at the Palace?"

Seth nodded.

"Good. Six o'clock in the lobby."

Cane gave his head a private shake. *No grass growing under Samantha Maples's toes.*

First Methodist Church
Buffalo, Wyoming Territory

The little white church on Adams Street had a quiet, welcoming intimate dignity about it. Longstreet's church experience for practical purposes ended on leaving the family plantation to go to war. Stepping inside with Maddie on his arm had a feeling unlike any other he remembered. Dark wooden pews marched up the central aisle on either side. Dimly lit silence scented in candle wax and furniture polish beckoned. It felt a place of refuge, a place to change his life with the woman who'd already changed his life. Reverend Austin awaited them at the head of the central aisle. Heels tatted to echoes as they made their way up the aisle.

"Mrs. O'Rourke and Mr. Longstreet, I presume, welcome."

"Thank you for seeing us, Reverend," Maddie said.

"Happy to discuss such a joyous occasion.

Please have a seat."

They took seats in two front pews.

"Maddie tells me this is your first marriage, Mr. Longstreet."

"It is. Please call me Beau."

"Very well, Beau. Marriage is a big step. You've waited more than a few years for yours."

Beau locked an eye in Maddie's. "Never came across the right woman before."

"I understand she had some reservation at your original proposal."

"Reservation? She ran off to Buffalo without leaving a trace."

"I'd call that a rejection. What changed?"

"My actions weren't so much rejection. I was afraid to accept."

"Why afraid?"

"My line of work, Reverend. I'm in law enforcement. It can be dangerous. Maddie lost her first husband. She didn't want to risk losing another."

"What changed?"

"I came to realize I'd lost the very man I was afraid of losing."

"I see by the star you wear, Beau, you're still in law enforcement."

"Beau is planning to run for sheriff this fall," Maddie said.

"And how did this reconciliation come about?"

"I sent for him amid all the recent troubles with the Stock Growers Association." She favored Beau with a smile and a wistful glance. "And he came."

"Love. It's been known to move mountains. I don't know if I have ever had the pleasure to unite two people in Holy Matrimony better suited to the institution you are about to enter into. Now about the arrangements."

Palace Hotel
Denver

She floated down the staircase to the lobby, hourglass figure full of promise. Blue-black curls, violet eyes, fine porcelain features, delicate lips fetching a hint at some private humor. Seth's limited experience with women left him awkward and ill-prepared for an apparition like this.

She smiled, looping her arm in his. "So glad we could do this before you have to leave."

"Uh-huh."

"Relax, handsome; Samantha doesn't bite."

"Good to hear. For a moment there I was worried."

She shot him a sidelong glance with one of those private smiles. "Found our footing, have we? Good."

She led him to a corner table in the lounge.

"Whiskey?"

"I would have thought sherry."

"I've been known to. I'm also known to be unpredictable." She signaled the waiter. "Two bourbons. So, what do I need to know about Seth Adams, starting with that curious little scar at the corner where you smile?"

"Old bear wrestling injury."

She laughed, a throaty laugh as the waiter set down their drinks. "Let me guess. You've worked with Longstreet."

"One case."

She lifted her glass in toast. "You learn fast."

"I've been told." He touched the rim of his to hers.

"Overlooking the bear, give me the rest."

"Kansas boy. Took to lawing up in Cheyenne. Beau liked what he saw on the case we worked. He suggested the Colonel consider me to replace him when he decided to stay on in Buffalo. Here I am."

"Here you are indeed. Could have predicted that."

"Predicted me coming here?"

"No, Beau staying on in Buffalo."

"How so?"

"Let's say I was Beau's marriage counselor."

"You know a lot about marriage?"

"Never been. That's what qualifies me to counsel those so inclined."

"I'm confused."

"We're off to a good start." She drained her glass and signaled the waiter. Two more.

"Your turn."

"Been with Pinkerton five years. Mr. Pinkerton finds women well suited to investigative work. We can be disarming, you see."

"I see. I believe I've been disarmed."

"Even better, you know it. Worked out of Chicago up to now. Reggie had enough call on me they transferred me here."

"Reggie?"

"Reginald Kingsley. Heads the Denver office. You'll likely meet him in due course."

Fresh drinks arrived.

"Now if you are to take Beau's place, we'll finish our drinks, and you'll buy me some supper."

"My pleasure."

"We'll see."

"See what?"

"We'll see if you actually take Beau's place."

As they left the lounge on the way to the dining room, Samantha paused, arrested by a dark gaze at the bar.

"Evening, Sam."

"Trevor."

"Working late?"

"Fraternizing."

"Anyone I should know?"

"If you must. Seth Adams, meet Trevor Travane, a colleague at Pinkerton."

"Ah, colleague, of course."

"Nice to meet you, Trevor." Seth extended his hand. Travane took it.

"Seth is moving to Denver too. He'll be replacing Beau Longstreet at Colonel Crooks's little league."

Seth took Travane's measure. Tall and lean, he moved with the fluid grace of an athlete. Dark, wavy hair, deep-brown eyes, and crisply hewn features gave the man a rakishly handsome appearance. The banter suggested "colleague" might understate the case.

"What's become of Beau?"

"Maddie O'Rourke finally collared him."

"Can't say I'm aggrieved."

"Didn't expect you would be. Seth and I were just on our way to dinner if you'll excuse us."

"No excuse needed."

Sam set off on Seth's arm.

"Nice to meet you, Trevor."

"You too, Seth."

CHAPTER THIRTY-THREE

U. P. Denver to Cheyenne
Smitten. Curious word he'd heard some-where. Never quite understood the notion. This must be something of it. *Samantha Maples. Pinkerton agent for gosh sakes.* The front range scrolled by the west window. Seth let his thoughts wander.

Dinner conversation jumbled together. She teased him about his awkward moments. For some reason, he enjoyed it. She said she was Beau's marriage counselor. Never been married, didn't sound like experience for counseling, unless her counsel ran against it. Might be more to it than that. She had a knack for understatement. Travane she said was a colleague. The look he gave her said a bit more than that. Understandable though given the direction his own thoughts were taking him. Possibilities. Samantha Maples had more than her share. He doubted she'd mind if she knew his thoughts ran along those lines. Lines all curved.

Desert he reckoned might have gone farther than the slice of apple pie they shared. Something about the look in her eye and that teasing way of hers. At the last she'd patted him on the cheek and said "Sweet." What's a fella to make of that? Smitten, might make a man sweet on a woman. Denver it seemed offered something more than a new job. *Unpredictable* she said. Not so sure about that. Samantha Maples might be more than predictable. It might be wishful thinking, but likely Beau Longstreet or Trevor Travane could set him straight. He'd not ask. He'd leave that up to Sam. "Come see me when you get back to Denver" she said. He said he would, and he would.

Sheriff's Office
Cheyenne
Seth found Sheriff Tyler at his desk when he returned to the office. Tyler greeted him with a knowing smile.

"How was Denver?"

"How'd you know I went to Denver?"

"Just a guess."

"We need to talk, Sheriff."

"Let's see, Colonel Crook offered you a

job with the league and you're moving to Denver."

"How do you know that?"

"Been expecting it since you got paid out on the bank fraud case. Took it for certain when I heard Beau Longstreet was fixin' to stay in Buffalo."

"I came back to work things out with you. Didn't promise Colonel Crook to be there before the first of next month."

"Appreciate that."

"And I appreciate all you done for me, takin' me on like you did. I learned a lot."

"Did a good job too. You earned your new opportunity. I'll get busy lookin' for a new deputy. In the meantime, you can welcome yourself back by makin' the rounds."

MC Ranch
Johnson County

McGant and Hardy rode in just before sunset. They put up their horses in the barn and set off for the ranch house. McGant broke out a bottle of whiskey and glasses while the cook rustled up steak, biscuits, and gravy. He poured two glasses and spread a map of Johnson County on the dining table.

"You notice the flashy buckskin in the corral when we rode in?"

"Hard not to. Why?"

" 'Cause you're gonna steal him. Well not exactly you. Dan Shaw's gonna steal him."

"Who's Dan Shaw?"

"Another score needs settling."

"Not sure I follow."

"Try this. We ride up to Buffalo tomorrow. You circle west and north around town with the buckskin while I ride in. The Shaw Ranch is northeast of town about here on French Creek." He tapped the map with his finger. "You ride in, and offer to sell the buckskin to Shaw. When you get your shot, kill him. Put the buckskin up in Shaw's corral and wait. I'll ride into Buffalo and report the theft of my horse to Whitaker. I'll tell him I seen Dan Shaw do it and followed him. I'll ride out to the Shaw place with the sheriff. You know what to do. You make smoke in the wind. I got a cinch tight alibi."

"Smart. Two birds, two fees, half now."

"I understand. I'll meet you back here to settle up."

Sheriff's Office
Buffalo

Buck McGant barged through the office door to find Sheriff Whitaker at his desk with Longstreet at his shoulder.

"Sheriff."

"Mr. McGant."

A flash of recollection washed over McGant's face. "What's he doin' here?"

"Beau Longstreet is my new deputy. What's on your mind?"

"Horse theft. Dan Shaw stole my champion buckskin stud."

"That don't sound a'tall like Dan. What makes you think it was him?"

"Saw him. Followed him. That horse is likely standing tall in his corral as we speak. I came here so as not to be seen takin' the law into my own hands here in Johnson County."

"Commendable citizenship."

"Are we going to lollygag here all day or are we going to ride out to the Shaw Ranch, recover my property, and arrest the thief?"

"We'll ride out there, soon as I tidy up a couple things and fetch my horse from the livery."

"You want me to ride along, Sheriff?"

"No, Beau. We're due to make rounds. You best do it."

Longstreet left the office to McGant fuming while Whitaker shuffled paper. He collected Yankee at a hitchrack in the next block and lit out of town for the Shaw Ranch.

Shaw Ranch

Dan watched Longstreet pound up the road from town on a lathered Yankee. He slid to a stop and jumped down.

"What on earth's after you?"

"Cole Hardy, most likely and he's after you."

"Who's Cole Hardy?"

"One of McGant's hired guns."

"McGant again. What's he up to this time?"

"Accusing you of stealing a prize stud of his."

"I don't know anything about his prize stud."

"I expect Cole Hardy does. Now let's get me and Yankee here out of sight."

Thirty minutes later a rough-shaved hard-case rode in on a long-striding bay, leading a solid built buckskin stallion.

Dan greeted him at the corral gate. "What can I do for you, stranger?"

"Got a horse for sale."

"Which one?"

"This buckskin here."

"Fine lookin' animal. Why would you want to sell him?"

"Bad run of cards. I need cash."

Dan looked the horse over. "Got a MC

brand on him. You got a bill of sale?"

"Course I do. Wouldn't be honest if I didn't."

"How much you want for him?"

"Hundred fifty."

"Best I can do is a hundred."

"Next to horse stealin', but I'll take it." Hardy stepped down.

"Let's turn him loose in the corral." Dan turned to the corral gate.

Hardy reached for his gun.

"I wouldn't do that if I were you." Longstreet stepped out of the barn, cocking his pistol leveled at Hardy. "Now drop it."

He did.

"What do we do with him for now?" Dan said.

"Get his gun. Then we tie him, gag him, and lock him up in the tack room."

"What then?"

"Then we wait for his boss."

Longstreet kept watch on the road up from town. It was near an hour later when he saw the first dust sign. McGant must have been fit to soil himself with Whitaker taking his time like he did. With Dan out of sight there was no one in the yard save the buckskin in the corral. Longstreet watched them ride in from the shadows of the barn door.

"See there, Sheriff. There's my buckskin. Just like I said. MC brand and all, see."

They stepped down.

"Dan," Whitaker called.

Longstreet stepped out of the shadows. "Dan's dead, Sheriff. I got here too late."

"Who killed him?"

"Ask Mr. McGant here. I believe he knows."

"I don't know what you're talkin' about."

"Oh, but you do. Man's name is Cole Hardy. You hired him to kill Dan and Sheriff Whitaker here."

"That's crazy talk."

"Is it? See I got here in time to apprehend him. Talkative fella when he feels the need. Matter of fact I got him tied down like a spring calf ready for branding. Never knew a calf to sing like that. You're under arrest, McGant. Accessory to murder. Likely get you life to a necktie party for that."

McGant went for his gun.

Longstreet's Colt barked, knocking the big rancher down in the dirt. Whitaker stomped his gun hand and relieved him of the pistol.

Blood leaked from McGant's shoulder wound. "I need a doctor."

"In due course," Whitaker said.

Longstreet holstered his gun. "You can

317

come out now, Dan. It's over."

"Ain't over for either of you, you too, Longstreet."

"Maybe so McGant, but it is over for you and Hardy. Attempted murder is a serious charge. I expect you'll be going away for quite a spell at a facility not quite up to Cattlemen's Club standards."

"Johnson County kangaroo court? I don't think so."

"We'll see," Whitaker said. "Come on, Beau, let's take these two birds in."

CHAPTER THIRTY-FOUR

League Office
Denver

Monday morning came with a hint of chill in the air. Seth took himself off to the office early. He waited for Colonel Crook to arrive at the opening.

"Seth, didn't expect to see you until next week."

"Sheriff Tyler was able to hire a new deputy sooner than we thought. Nothing holding me to Cheyenne. I thought I'd get myself down here and get started."

"Glad you did. Come on in." Unlocking the door Crook led them inside. "Beau used the desk on the right, back by the window. It's yours now. Take stock and let me know if you need anything."

Seth walked the aisle between two rows of desks to the one with a window to the street. He tried the barrel-back chair on for size. He rocked back. He found paper in one desk drawer and a pencil in another. Tools of the trade along with a pair of new pearl bird's-head grip, nickel-plated Colts. A .41 caliber Thunderer with a five-inch barrel rode low on his right hip, holstered in a stylish black rig. He carried a matching Colt Lightning, chambered .38 for a four-inch barrel, shoulder rigged beneath his coat on the left. He'd ordered the pair with some of the reward money he picked up following the bank fraud case. Welcome to the Great Western Detective League.

"See you found your way back." Cane strode down the aisle to his desk.

"Mornin', Briscoe. I did."

"Didn't think we'd see you quite so soon."

"Sheriff Tyler found himself a deputy sooner than we expected."

"Good for him and for us. Welcome."

"Thanks, glad to be here."

"Let me know if you need anything."

"You mentioned you may know of a room available."

"I do. If you're going to take over Longstreet's desk, you might as well have his room too. I'll take you by after work."

"Thanks."

"Briscoe, Seth, come in please." Crook waved from his office door. "Stack of dodgers come in overnight. We should probably have a look."

They rose from their desks and started up the aisle to Crook's office. Cane took note of Seth's new pistol.

"Nice rig. Makes a statement."

"My old single action army needed replacing. After the reward on the bank fraud case I could afford it. This little beauty too." He drew back his coat.

"Smart. Backup comes in handy."

Seth followed Cane into the office and took one of the chairs drawn up before the desk. Crook slid a stack of wanted dodgers across the desk to Cane. Briscoe studied the first and passed it to Seth.

"What are we looking for?"

Crook took up the question. "These are men and occasionally a woman wanted by one or more of the league offices. We circulate the dodgers to familiarize the members with who they should be on the lookout for. Once in a while a member may recognize someone known to be in their area. It doesn't happen often, but the collars come quick."

The stack passed one by one. Most were rough looking hardcases. Seth paused over one.

"Look familiar?" Crook said.

"Slick looker. Reminds me of Prather."

"The crooked bank president?"

"Yeah. Not him, but a man like this could stand out in a crowd." He handed the wanted poster to Crook.

"Gideon Rival. Wanted for counterfeiting. Suits him. I see what Longstreet saw in your savvy."

O'Rourke House

Cane paused before a stately Victorian on a quiet tree-lined street.

"This is it. Abigale Fitzwalter is the proprietress. Tell her you're the young man I spoke to her about."

"You comin' too?"

"After five. Time I find my way home."

"Where's that?"

"Silver Slipper Saloon."

"You live in a saloon?"

"Upstairs. Makes for a short walk after I slack my thirst and have a bite to eat. All the comforts of home without havin' to make 'em myself."

Seth shook his head.

"Beau didn't understand it either. He went this route. Ended up married."

"Am I risking that?"

"Don't think so. Leastwise not with Mrs. Fitzwalter. See ya in the mornin'."

Cane took himself back down the block

toward town. Seth climbed the steps to a broad front porch. He knocked on a door with leaded glass windows and lace curtains.

A heavyset woman with a mound of steel gray hair piled on the top of her head fringed here and there with errant strands escaped from the pile.

"May I help you?"

"Mrs. Fitzwalter, Seth Adams. Briscoe Cane suggested I see you about the possibility of a room."

"Ah, so you're the young man, just moved here from Cheyenne."

"Yes, ma'am."

"Please, come in and do call me Abigail."

The polished foyer was flanked by a dining room on the left and a parlor on the right. A central staircase ascended to the upper floors beside a hallway leading to the back of the house.

"Let's have a seat in the parlor and get acquainted."

Seth took a wing chair while Abigail composed herself on the settee.

"I understand you will be joining Colonel Crook's detective association."

"Yes ma'am. Did today."

"Abigail."

"Sorry."

"Beau Longstreet lived here for a number

of years. His room is the one I have available."

"Seems like I'm taking his place in more ways than one, starting with his desk today."

"I'm so happy for both Beau and Maddie. Near broke his heart after she left following that dreadful abduction business."

"Abduction?"

"Long story. Best left for another time. Now about the room. You should be aware there are certain rules observed in this house. You should be familiar with them before you consider taking a room. Breakfast is served at seven, dinner at six-thirty. No female guests are permitted beyond the parlor. No gambling or late-night carousing on the premises. Strong drink is permitted only in moderation and I am the sole judge of moderation. Does that sound acceptable?"

"Yes . . . Abigail."

"Good, come along. I'll show you the room."

He followed her to the stairs for the climb.

"It's on the third floor. A bit of a hike but it's usually quiet up there."

The room was large and airy with windows on two sides. The furnishings were comfortably simple with a small writing desk, a wing chair, armoire, washbasin, and bed.

"The rent is twenty dollars a month with one month on deposit in advance. Is that acceptable?"

"This will do nicely." He fished two twenty-dollar gold-pieces out of his pocket. "If you don't mind, I'll spend the night and bring what few things I have over tomorrow."

"I'll set an extra place for supper. Welcome to O'Rourke House, Seth."

CHAPTER THIRTY-FIVE

League Office
Denver

The clock on the office wall crawled toward lunchtime. It started as a faint familiar hint of a sound. A merry little melody, swelling a block up the street. Distinctive, joyous, a calliope announcing a circus come to town. The little boy in Seth tugged him out of his desk, out of the office, and up the street to the sound, gathering a crowd.

The lead wagon was drawn by a high-stepping, four-in-hand matched team of white draft horses. The gold-guilt red wagon bore the steam-tooting instrument played by a man in a gold-trimmed red coat with a tall hat bearing a feathered plum plume at the crown. As the wagon passed, townsfolk poured out of shops and offices, gathering spontaneous crowds on both sides of the street.

A parade of brightly colored wagons

drawn by equally handsome teams followed with fearsome lions and tigers, lolling about their cages in sleepy disinterest. Clowns played to the crowds on both sides of the street, eliciting excited giggles from children and smiles from even the most jaundiced observers. A gaggle of performers came along next. Scantily clad painted aerial act artists, trick riders standing on saddle pads or astride a pair of prancing matched blacks. A small brass band blared a stirring march with the end of the parade punctuated by a beautiful woman seated atop a plodding pachyderm bedecked in a jeweled head harness. This last followed by a roustabout pushing a wheelbarrow armed with a shovel against any waste refuse as might be left behind.

"That's called bringing up the rear."

The voice at his elbow instantly recognizable.

"Hi, handsome. Welcome to Denver."

Samantha, stunning as ever. "Been to the circus?"

"Not since I was a little girl."

"Like to go?"

She smiled. "I was on my way to lunch."

"So was I."

"Care to join me? We can discuss this circus proposal of yours."

Proposal. Not so understated that.

Bank of Denver
The bank lobby emptied out for the parade coming by. Everyone, including Bank of Denver cashier Everett Ellis, joined the throng, watching the circus acts go by the boardwalk. Ellis's attention was torn away from an attractive aerial artist by a tall, well-dressed stranger who entered the bank. Ellis stepped back inside.

"Welcome to Bank of Denver, sir. How may we be of service?"

He held up a one-hundred-dollar gold certificate. "Need change for this."

"Right this way." Ellis stepped behind the nearest teller counter.

The stranger passed a crisp new bill over the counter. Ellis picked it up.

"Don't get many this large, never mind this new."

"Picked it up bucking the tiger. Other than faro they're not much good for day-to-day use."

Ellis felt the paper, laid the bill on the counter beside the teller drawer and a twenty-dollar gold certificate, judging the ink. "They aren't much good for day-to-day use and this one isn't even good for faro." He handed the bill back to the stranger.

"What do you mean?"

"It's counterfeit."

"The hell it is. I won it fair and square at the Golden Nugget."

"Then you should have cashed your chips in gold nuggets, 'cause this paper isn't worth the ink it's printed in."

The stranger slammed the bill back on the counter. "I say you're wrong. This note is as good as the mint printed it."

"Somebody printed it, but it wasn't no mint. Sorry to be the bearer of bad tidings, but it would appear you've been swindled."

"Damn it! This here's legal tender. This is a bank. You're obliged to cash it."

"If it were legal tender, we'd cash it. It's not. Now if you'll excuse me, sir."

Ellis returned to his desk, disappointed to have missed the rest of the show.

The stranger stormed out of the lobby as customers and staff filed back in at the end of the parade.

Twenty minutes later, head teller Matilda Morris approached Ellis's desk.

"Excuse me, Everett, I was counting vault cash when the parade started. Did you return it to the vault by any chance?"

"Vault cash? No. Where was it?"

"Last teller station nearest the vault."

"How much?"

"I'd finished four bundles of a thousand dollars each."

"Let's have a look. Is it possible it became mislaid somehow?"

"I don't see how."

"We'll have to audit the vault. What denominations were you working with?"

"Twenties."

Home Cookin' Café

They took a corner booth and ordered two blue-plate specials. Your choice piece of fried chicken, breast for Samantha, leg and thigh for Seth, with mashed potatoes, wilted greens, and steaming mugs of coffee.

"When did you get back to town?"

"Last week."

"Did you find a place to stay?"

"Briscoe lined me up with a room at O'Rourke House."

"Nice place. Stayed there for a time myself once. Didn't work out though."

"Oh, why not?"

"Longstreet, Maddie O'Rourke, and me all under the same roof? You figure it out. Crook got you working on anything yet?"

"Just learning the ropes."

"You?"

"Suspicious wife with a philandering husband. Cupidity cases are boring. Too simple."

"How so?"

She lifted her lashes over a forkful of mashed potato, "Same reason I didn't work out living at O'Rourke House. So, were you serious?"

"Serious about what?"

"Going to the circus."

"I was. Haven't seen one since I was in knee-britches."

"Couldn't have been that long ago. Warn you, I'm an expensive circus date."

Seth lifted a brow.

"Popcorn?"

"I think I can handle it."

"Might be dinner after."

"I'll take you up on that."

"Glutton for punishment."

"They have cherry pie for dessert."

They never made it to dessert. A man in a bowler hat with a cane entered the restaurant and made straight for their booth.

"Thought I might find you here. Samantha, a word if I might?"

"Of course. Seth, this Reginald Kingsley, managing director in Denver's Pinkerton office. Reggie, meet Seth Adams, Crook's newest."

"Ah, the one to look after Longstreet's piece. Pleased to meet you." He offered his hand. "We shall have to get acquainted, perhaps over drinks some time. At the moment I'm afraid I must have a word with Samantha."

They stepped a discreet distance away. Little about Reginald Kingsley spoke of a Pinkerton operative, much less master detective. He had the pinched appearance of a librarian or college professor with alert blue eyes, aquiline features, and a full mustache tinged in the barest hint of gray. He favored wool jackets in subdued hues, herringbone in this case. The silver tipped cane he might wield as a baton or break into a rapier-like blade. In the field, he armed himself with a short barreled .44 Colt pocket pistol cradled in a shoulder holster. He could disappear in a crowd or turn himself out in a chameleon of disguise to suit his purpose. He dripped comfortable British charm, easily insinuating himself into the trust of the unsuspecting criminal or soon to be informant.

Conversation finished, he headed for the door. Samantha returned to the booth. "Afraid I'll have to take a rain check on the pie."

"Trouble?"

"Seems the Bank of Denver misplaced four-thousand dollars while arguing with a stranger over cashing a counterfeit bill. Sounds like a diversion. What do I owe you for lunch?"

"I'll take care of it."

She patted his cheek. "You're a love." And was gone.

Counterfeit. Gideon Rival's dodger image appeared in Seth's mind. In the middle of a circus parade no less.

CHAPTER THIRTY-SIX

Fairgrounds

Call it a hunch. It clearly couldn't be any more than that. The fairgrounds were located on the east end of town. With setup underway Seth walked into a hive of activity. Roustabouts busied themselves with erecting the big top. Canvas and hemp scented the air mingled with strong animal smell. Heavy hammers thudded stout pegs in hard ground. An elephant, tacked to erect the central pole, stood patiently by browsing hay. Everywhere performers and handlers tended their animals. Seth set off south around the perimeter, looking.

Looking for what? Something or someone out of place. A red-haired woman, painted in revealing tights, looked him up and down with undisguised interest. He smiled to himself. *Already got a date for the circus.* He guessed asking might win a private performance. Sideshows occupied the perimeter with colorful tents or wagons offering all manner of wonders. For the pittance of a dime or a nickel you could view a bearded lady, a man-eating snake, or a tattooed lady with tattoos where a lady shouldn't be viewed. Go ahead. Find something out of place in this menagerie.

The east sideshows offered games of chance. Here five cents or a dime might earn your child or your sweetheart a prize. Two bits might win a pocket watch or a cameo brooch of European worth, whatever that might be. More oddities came next. The Strong Man would treat you to unimaginable feats of Herculean strength. Next came Tiny Man who once used a teacup for his crib. Seth caught up short. The well-dressed man beside the tent with the little man. Well-dressed. Slipped something in his coat pocket. Seth feigned interest in the Strong Man's wagon, watching.

The man turned to go. Gideon Rival stood out, out of place on a circus lot. What was it the Tiny Man had given him? Time enough for that later. He followed Rival down the midway toward town. Rival headed for the Palace Hotel. Seth caught up to him when he paused to light a cheroot. The Lightning cleared leather from his coat.

"Gideon Rival, hands up. You're under arrest."

Rival lifted his hands. Seth claimed a derringer from his vest pocket.

"On what charge?"

"Counterfeiting is on your wanted dodger. Depending on what's in your coat pocket we may add bank robbery to the charge. Sheriff's office is just up the block there on the right. Move."

Ten minutes later, Gideon Rival cooled his heels in a jail cell. His coat pocket yielded two bank bundles of one-thousand dollars each. Seth and the sheriff walked back to the fairgrounds to have a chat with the Tiny Man, which turned up two more bundles before Tiny Man reunited with Rival in the next cell.

Bank of Denver

Everett Ellis checked his pocket watch. Two minutes to three. Closing time. He glanced at Reginald Kingsley and Samantha Maples.

"Excuse me for a moment while I close up."

He was just about to flip the open sign to closed when a young man opened the door.

"I'm sorry, sir. We're just closing."

Seth held up four bank bundles of cash. "I expect you're still looking for these."

"Where did you get that?"

"From the thieves."

"Who are you?"

"Seth Adams," Samantha said with a spark of mirth in her eye an incredulous Reggie Kingsley didn't catch.

"Great Western Detective League," Seth added.

"Colonel Crook's outfit."

"Yes, sir."

"But how did you know? We sent for the Pinkertons."

"I know. Sam and I were having lunch when she got the call from Mr. Kingsley."

Kingsley looked at Samantha. "What did you tell him?"

"All I said was the bank had an attempt to pass a counterfeit bill."

Reggie turned to Seth. "And from that you got a recovery?"

"That and a hunch."

"I don't follow."

"We had a dodger on one Gideon Rival in the office this morning. Wanted for counterfeiting."

"He couldn't have stolen the money," Ellis said. "He never left my sight."

"He had an accomplice."

"He couldn't have. We were the only two people in the bank."

337

"There was a third alright. You just didn't see him."

"Impossible."

"Mind if I have a look around?"

Ellis stepped aside, a sweeping bow of approval. Seth walked along the teller line toward the vault.

"Where was the money when it was taken?"

"Last teller station nearest the vault."

Seth reached the end of the counter. A side door to the alley opened between the teller back counter and the vault.

"Here's your problem."

"That door is always locked."

"Picked."

"If anyone had come in that way, I would have seen him."

"Not if he was three feet tall."

"What?"

"The counterfeit bill was a diversion. The circus was another. Rival's accomplice was the circus Tiny Man."

Kingsley shook his head. "How in the Queen's name did you put all that together?"

"I had a hunch. The circus commotion was just too convenient. I went looking for Rival. Found him with the Tiny Man. Followed him. Pinched him. The sheriff and I collected his little friend. They're both guests of the county and the bank has its money back."

"I suspect the directors shall wish to reward you Mr. . . . Adams is it?"

"Seth Adams."

Under the Big Top

Samantha had popcorn on her nose and an impish grin.

"Reggie was apoplectic. Speechless if you can imagine. Never seen him so."

"Apo . . ."

"Furious. He hates to lose. Have a recovery snatched out from under his nose before he even finished interviewing the client. You can't imagine. And for what? A one-word clue and a hunch. Do you do this sort of thing all the time?"

"Don't know. I just started."

"Popcorn?"

He took a pinch. "A little salty."

"So are my lips. You can fix that later."

She snuggled closer on the bench, gazing up at a man walking a wire high above the center ring.

Sunday Afternoon

Seth made the walk to O'Rourke House in something of a disoriented daze. Turned out

Sam had more needed fixin' than salty lips. After supper at Delmonico's he walked her to the Savoy Hotel. The Savoy wasn't the Palace, but as Samantha explained it was comfortable and affordable. She'd taken to staying there when she came to Denver on business. With her transfer to Denver she arranged with the owner to rent a room. They got to her door on the second floor and made a fine fix of her salty lip problem, which in truth he found anything but salty. That's when she insisted his tie was askew and in need of fixing. Before he knew what was happening everything came askew. Beautifully askew. Amazingly so.

This morning they'd had a leisurely breakfast in the hotel dining room, followed by what Sam insisted was a "proper 'til next time." Remarkable. Take that over a handshake anytime. She allowed as how "it'd be nice having him around." Nice? "Let's see what the week brings. Maybe drinks and dinner one night." He'd been a little breathless by that parting kiss. He thought he'd said yes.

What to make of this Samantha Maples creature? What indeed. Time would tell. In the meantime, he'd count the days.

First Methodist Church
Buffalo

Soft sepia light suffused the church, pews gleaming in polish. Candle wax with a floral hint scented the air. Longstreet stood at the foot of the altar at the head of the center aisle beside Dan Shaw. Reverend Austin took his place in the sanctuary behind them. Mrs. Austin struck up a familiar wedding processional as Susan Shaw started up the aisle. She wore a simple gray dress, holding a bunch of purple violets at her waist. She smiled, taking her place beside Dan.

Then there was Maddie. The moment caught in Longstreet's throat as he had never known a moment to catch. Auburn hair cascaded in soft waves down a stunning deep green gown. Freckle-splashed nose, cheeks blushing peaches. Green eyes glistening her lips composed a small smile touched with love.

Longstreet followed her down the aisle with his eyes. His mind raced back to those awkward days at O'Rourke House. Maddie and her rules. His mischievous bending those rules. Her attempts at insistence, slowly eroded. He remembered the day he realized he was comfortable there. Comfortable with her. It made her uncomfortable. He liked that. He passed over her parting.

She was here now. All that mattered in the moment. A moment forever.

She took his arm. They turned to Reverend Austin.

"Dearly beloved, we are gathered here today to join Madeline O'Rourke and Beauregard Longstreet in holy matrimony."

Maddie glanced up at Beau, nearly disbelieving it had come to this. He'd upset her self-contented widowhood almost from the moment she laid eyes on him. So much so she fought her feelings, near panic in desperate denial. Fought them only to fall in love. Fought them to flee for fear of losing him only to realize she'd lost him. Out of fear, she reached out to him. Out of love, he answered her call. And now she was to be his and he was to be hers. All as it should be.

"Maddie O'Rourke, do you take Beauregard Longstreet to be your lawfully wedded husband, to love and to cherish, in sickness and in health, until death do you part?"

A tear steaked the cheek she turned to him. "I do."

"And you Beauregard Longstreet, do you take Madeline O'Rourke to be your lawfully wedded wife, to love and to cherish, in sickness and in health, until death do you part?"

"I do."

"Then in the name of Jesus Christ, I pronounce you husband and wife. You may kiss the bride."

Time stood still in that moment as it always did for each one in the other.

O'Rourke House
Denver
1911

I closed my notebook and slipped it into my coat pocket. Briscoe sat quietly seemingly lost in some thought.

"How did they happen to come to our wedding?"

He came back to the present. "Beau retired from the sheriff's office in Buffalo. They decided to celebrate by paying Denver a visit. They happened to be here the day of your wedding. Angela and I invited them along. We didn't think you'd mind."

"Of course not. I might have missed out on this story if you hadn't invited them for us."

"Speaking of us, how are you doing with your new home?" Angela asked from the parlor doors.

I smiled. "Every week comes with some new lesson in home ownership. As of now it looks like I'll be going back into the furniture refinishing business."

"Splendid," her eyes brightened. "What will you be refinishing this time?"

The moment of truth had arrived as I knew it would. Nothing for it but the truth.

"A cradle."

"A cradle! For a baby?"

"Be a little small for much else."

"Oh, Robert! That's so exciting. Congratulations. Did you hear that, Briscoe? Robert and Penny are expecting."

"Ain't deef, dear. Course I heard it."

"Have you chosen any names yet?"

"Afraid not. I'm still getting used to the idea of me being a father. I've no doubt my Penny will be a wonderful mother; but me fathering a little one, I just don't know."

"Seems the fathering's already been done," Briscoe said. "Now it's the upbringing."

"Never mind what he says and not to worry, you'll be a wonderful father."

"Have you found a cradle yet?"

"No."

"Well when you do, bring it to the carriage house to refinish. That way Briscoe can help you and get him out from under my feet for a time."

I rose to the horrifying thought, *picking out names for a baby might be worse than furniture.*

AUTHOR'S NOTE

All cases featured in the Great Western Detective League Series have a basis in historical fact, though we take more fictional license with these stories than we do with our historical dramatizations. The league is loosely based on General David J. Cook's Rocky Mountain Detective Association, which operated across the west in the later decades of the nineteenth century, pursuing investigative innovations in law enforcement akin to those we imagine here. The bank robbery forgery case is based on an actual crime swiftly brought to justice by General Cook himself while he served as county sheriff.

Powder River Range is loosely based on the Johnson County War in northern Wyoming. Many of the events of this story took place during that conflict. Locations, organizations, and geography are consistent with historical fact as is the conflict between the open range cattle barons and those settling the land under the Homestead Act of 1862. The characters are fictional, though Nate Champion has a basis in history. The stand-off at his ranch didn't end quite as well as the one we portrayed. The assassin Tom Dorn is based on the legendary Tom Horn who did assassin work for the Stock Growers Association during the war.

Paul Colt

ABOUT THE AUTHOR

Paul Colt's critically acclaimed historical fiction crackles with authenticity. His analytical insight, investigative research, and genuine horse sense bring history to life. His characters walk off the pages of history with a blend of Jeff Shaara's historical dramatizations and Robert B. Parker's gritty dialogue. Paul Colt does action adventure western style. Paul's *Grasshoppers in Summer,* and *Friends Call Me Bat* are Western Writers of America Spur Award honorees. *Boots and Saddles: A Call to Glory* received the Marilyn Brown Novel Award, presented by Utah Valley University. Reviewers recognize Paul's lively, fast paced style, complex plots, and touches of humor. Readers say, *"Pick up a Paul Colt book, you can't put it down."* To learn more visit Facebook @paulcoltauthor

The employees of Thorndike Press hope you have enjoyed this Large Print book. All our Thorndike, Wheeler, and Kennebec Large Print titles are designed for easy reading, and all our books are made to last. Other Thorndike Press Large Print books are available at your library, through selected bookstores, or directly from us.

For information about titles, please call:
(800) 223-1244

or visit our website at:
gale.com/thorndike

To share your comments, please write:
Publisher
Thorndike Press
10 Water St., Suite 310
Waterville, ME 04901